The Old Prostitute and Other Stories

Manisha Roy

CHIRON PUBLICATIONS • ASHEVILLE, NORTH CAROLINA

www.ChironPublications.com

Cover image by Rhoda Kassof-Isaac
Interior and cover design by Danijela Mijailovic
Printed primarily in the United States of America.

ISBN 978-1-68503-091-9 paperback
ISBN 978-1-68503-092-6 hardcover
ISBN 978-1-68503-093-3 electronic
ISBN 978-1-68503-094-0 limited edition paperback

Library of Congress Cataloging-in-Publication Data Pending

For my two close friends
Portia and Trudy

Preface

How did I became a fiction writer—if not a famous one, at least a happy one? It is a personal story which demonstrates the transformative significance of synchronistic events in my life – a fact I realized only in retrospect many years later.

I was born in a small town of India, which was a British colony at the time. Our town was located at the foothills of the eastern Himalayas, close to the borders of Tibet and Myanmar and was the only place that produced petroleum for the whole country, making it a sophisticated industrial center where people from advanced technological parts of the world came to work. However, the town itself was surrounded by tropical forests inhabited by wild animals like elephants, rhinoceros and huge pythons. These surroundings no doubt had a lasting impact on me as a young girl who loved to take long walks along the hilly roads. I also liked to find secluded corners of the house and garden to read books especially during long school vacations in summer. My parents had a sizable library in our home and they were avid readers themselves. My mother was strict about what my older brother and I read and monitored our choice of books. I was curious about what she read and I was old enough to know that her books must hold something forbidden and juicy.

One summer when I was 13 years old, I stole my mother's keys when she was taking a nap. Her keys were always tied to the end of her sari and I had to be careful not to wake her. I used one of the keys to open the locked bookcase where all forbidden and mysterious books were kept. As I tried to take a novel out, a thin book fell from the back of that book. Curious I opened it and got interested enough to leave the novel alone and locked up the bookcase again and returned mother's keys to its place. I began to read the book which turned out to be a nonfiction memoir by a forest ranger who described his work and encounters in the forest so vividly and beautifully that I was hooked and finished the book in one sitting, away from the eyes of everyone. I was so mesmerized by this thin book that I promised myself that someday I must become a writer, a writer who can uplift the readers to a world of suspended disbelief with the help of enchanting stories created by beautiful magical language. Even at that age I knew that his pen was powerful enough to transform the forest into a character participating in the wonderful story he created. The thrill of this discovery kept me in a daze for days to come. Thus my love for literature was born and has accompanied me my whole life. I did not share this experience with anyone because I had a feeling it was a self-discovery that belonged to me alone.

After this incident the summer vacation came to an end and I became busy with my studies. I always kept a journal and I mentioned this book there but over the years I sort of forgot this particular incident because I was preoccupied with my academic ambition and worked hard to achieve that. After finishing high school I was awarded two scholarships to finish my college education. I left my birthplace at age 15 to go to college in one of the largest cities of the world 900 miles away from my town and six years later, after completing my first Master's degree, I left India altogether for the US to finish my doctorate. The next three decades were busy with finishing one more Master's and two postgraduate degrees. I also changed my career a couple of times and was proud of my intellectual achievements. I worked hard traveling all over the world teaching, lecturing and also treating patients in short-term therapy. The memoir *My Four Homes* describes these years in details.

Then on October 26,1994 I was hospitalized to have an angiogram because of mild symptoms of chest pain. I spent the night at the hospital. They wanted to do the test early the next morning. I slept badly that night because of occasional chest pain. Early morning the next day around six, the nurse asked me to take a shower to prepare for the procedure. As I was standing under the warm shower, I saw the autumn color on the trees outside the bathroom window. I had a strange sensation, as if I was watching myself going through a ritual of profound importance; the colorful trees of the season had something in common with the stage of my life. I was 58 years old.

During the angiogram I felt an enormous urge to sleep. It was a very pleasant sensation, as if I was sleeping after many sleep-less nights. I awoke some ten hours later after a quintuple coronary bypass surgery and was told that I had a massive heart attack while going through the angiogram! I was lucky to be in the hospital to receive an emergency surgery that saved my life. Following the surgery for two months I suffered excruciating pain and was in bed without any energy or desire to do anything, not even to listen to my favorite music. For the first time in my life I had a forced rest but such an invasive surgery on my heart pushed me into a long bout of painful depression. I refused to take any antidepressant and spent over a month of extremely difficult time. The only question that kept humming in my head was, "Why was I saved from a sure death. There must be a purpose to this fateful event."

Then one December morning – two months after my surgery - I woke up with a renewed energy and looked out the window to see a little Junko bird picking into a pile of snow for food. This most ordinary and simple image made me smile and like a flash I remembered the promise I made to myself when I was 13. There was absolutely no doubt in my mind that it was for that purpose I was given a second chance to live. The only dream that I could recall from the past two months was a brief image of my appointment book disappearing in the quick sand of a beach.

As soon as I recovered I changed my daily schedule. I cut down my practice to a quarter, changed my diet to heart-healthy food and continued to follow an exercise regimen. I also took over a dozen creative writing classes through the Harvard Extension program and elsewhere to make sure that I had the ability to become a writer. I was assured by all the teachers that I could do it. As I kept doing the class exercises, I relived some of the feelings born during my solitary walks in my beautiful town when I wove daydreams and created many stories in my head. The habit of telling stories began early in my life. While walking back from my school nearly two miles I had a group of friends as my captive audience whom I told stories I read or listened to when our father read English books to us on winter Sundays under a warm quilt. If I saw a Disney movie for children, I told my friends the stories, embellishing as I pleased.

During the last part of the Second World War, our family visited our grandparents in the safety of the country side to escape the Japanese bombs. That was a year of memorable days and nights full of games, fun and stories. Many of the relatives gathered in our grandparents' home. There were over fifteen cousins between the ages of 5 and 20. My grandmother told me and her other grandchildren the mythological tales of the Hindu pantheon. We were glued to her in the evenings to travel to those divine worlds where the gods and their adversaries had their adventures. Listening and telling stories were a natural part of my upbringing. To this day, I see stories scattered all around me. So, to be a fiction writer was a natural wish I nurtured – unconsciously for 45 years until a severe health crisis made it conscious. It was as if the unconscious needed to bring the message via a life-threatening wake-up call otherwise the ego would not listen. I mentioned already the only brief dream I had during my long recovery. What a simple statement from the unconscious to tell me that I had to stop so many of my professional and social engagements.

I was intoxicated with my successful academic career. Yet, on some level I knew that I could not be happy on a deeper sense unless I became a fiction-writer. Otherwise I could not work that hard at it. I also began to write in my mother tongue – the language of the book that mesmerized me and the language of my mother and grandmother who told me my first stories. In 2001 while I was in India for a holiday, I began to write a memoir in Bengali and finished it in three months. It flowed out of me like a spring flood. It was published in India followed by a raving review. The same book was translated later by me and was published in this country in 2015 by Chiron under the title *My Four Homes*.

Speaking of my books, every one of them followed some kind of professional or personal crisis. My first field-research in early 60s as an anthropology student was among a remote hill tribe of the same state where I was born. Within the first month of my encounter with these people, I realized I could not remain objective – an academic expectation all graduate students of anthropology were trained to fulfill. I betrayed my hard-earned training and kept a separate journal of what attracted me more than recording the so-called objective facts on the ground. Years later that side journal became a book of true stories titled *The Reckoning Heart* where I had to reckon with what kind of anthropologist I'd like to be. My most successful book, the revised version of my doctoral dissertation, *Bengali Women*, was another journal that I kept when I moved to the big city of Kolkata from my birth town of 2000 people. My observations of human interactions were so alien and full of surprises to me that I had to record them.

Looking back, I see how my creative writing acted as a bridge between my conscious concerns and questions and my relationship to my unconscious archetypal world. The primary question that kept at me most of my anthropological career was the nature of the connection between an individual's culture and her life – how much cultural conditioning shapes an individual's aspirations and values? Can one's cultural teachings be the appropriate conduit for the emotional and spiritual fulfillments? I believe all my books try to answer these questions indirectly because these have been my questions throughout my life. In a way, the fictional characters that I create are various embodiments of the same questions. These particular questions have been important for me because I lived over 65 years in other cultures away from my own. As I age I realize that my adaptation to other cultures remains limited and on a deeper level I remain connected to my native culture via what I call cultural archetypes like language, art, food and early relationships.

I tried to capture this experience in my latest novel through the experiences of the main characters. The protagonist Charles Hamilton had no understanding of his own nature to have the ability to read people from another country. His good intention to help eradicate the parasitic diseases in India was incidental to accomplishing his own research. His opus was ego-driven to advance his career. Naturally, he was faced with one impediment after another.

When I write, I am totally absorbed in the story; the characters are always with me. I walk with them, have tea with them, have hours of conversations with them. They become my inner family and friends. Later I realize that I am engaged in a kind of "active imagination" to get to know and hopefully integrate my shadow figures both positive and negative. Thus a serious act of creative writing can be likened to deep analysis. At least that's the way I experience my writing. Otherwise, I could not have worked so hard at it. I wrote, rewrote, revised and proofread each of my 8 books at least five times and the three books I co-edited took even more work. If writing for me were not my soul work, I could not have done it so long and so hard.

Before ending I need to say a few words about translating myself. I have translated one memoir and several short stories from Bengali to English. What I noticed is that the act of translation helps me to revisit my life-long multi-cultural living experience. Each time I translate my own writing, I realize how I may be able to make a particular foreign experience my own while leaving another alone. Understanding another culture is possible only up to a point. Those of us who chose life's partners from another culture eventually revisit the same challenge mentioned above. But that's another whole topic.

However, because we all share the collective unconscious our intuitive understanding goes a long way. That's why a psychologically sensitive writer cannot judge situations and characters in another culture fully because they know that's a convenient occasion of projection. Yet a successful writer is able to create a villain who may be able to melt some readers' hearts. Nowhere am I reminded of this more than when I create different characters in a story. Without a pluralistic and non-judgmental approach I cannot create authentic characters. This exercise is somewhat similar to an analyst's acceptance of her clients without judgment. For that, the author herself must be authentic.

For me personally the questions I have been trying to answer by writing fiction also includes my need to be a global citizen and to learn how to reconcile my personal concerns with the serious and urgent concerns of our planet today. It's a constant struggle but I take Carl Jung's words to heart and try to remain steadfast in my miniscule way to serve the global society with whatever small power I have. In my private life I try not to abuse the depleting natural resources and teach my fictional characters, if not my relatives, to do the same. Naturally I'm more successful with the first group.

Manisha Roy

Table of Contents

Mother Country

The Old Prostitute

Kanakbala picks up her pet dog in her arms and gets ready to go for a walk along the river as she does everyday. She wraps her black-bordered white sari around carefully and quickly glances at the tiny mirror hung on the wall from a nail. She does not take time to focus on her face because she knows that the face that will look back at her is one she no longer recognizes. It's a different face than the beautiful one she has known, loved and was proud of all her life. Her current face has so many lines it looks like a piece of paper on which a child has scribbled intersecting lines again and again. Her hair has gone gray awhile back. Looking at this face now, Kanak finds it hard to believe that in the past the spell of her beauty attracted so many gentlemen. It caused her female neighbors to burn with jealousy.

Kanak and a dozen women live in a line of asbestos-roofed huts on a piece of fallow land that runs along the edge of the village and ending in a narrow river where nothing but dwarf weeds grow in clumps. A few bushes of wildflowers may come up in spring. The villagers rarely come this way even though a narrow walk runs along the fallow land leading to the village market. This river without a name shrinks into a drain during the dry winter season but swells into a river after the monsoon in summer. The inhabitants of the huts use its water the year round for washing and swimming.

Kanak was born in one of these huts seventy-nine years back. When Kanak's mother became pregnant, she retired from her inherited livelihood and moved away to the other side of the village intending to give her daughter a respectable life. But before Kanak was five, her mother died of malaria. Before she died, she urged one of her old neighbors to take care of her daughter, but made her promise to help her daughter find a respectable life. Being the only child in the whole neighborhood, Kanak received plenty of affection and food and grew up a happy woman with a beauty that reminded everyone of her beautiful mother. Her adopted mother did not waste the prospect of a good income and initiated Kanak into the same profession despite Kanak's mother's dying request to the contrary. Then one day Kanak's adopted mother also became old and left this world, leaving Kanak alone. Kanak cried for many days sitting near the river casting her eyes across the water wondering if other people also lose not one but two mothers in one lifetime. Then she took a dip in the river and came to her mother's hut and dressed in one of her mother's saris and joined others in earning her living. How else could she survive?

Days, months and years rolled on. Kanak has had a successful profession way into her 60s. At age 65 after an incident, she suddenly dropped out of her work. She had a regular client who visited her once every week. That evening was reserved for him. In that one evening she earned enough for the whole month. Then the news circulated that the rich client's wife died of a heart attack and afterward he never stepped foot in Kanak's neighborhood. Kanak confided in her friends that she fell in love with this client, and he promised to marry her one day and take her far away from the village to the big city where they would live together forever. All this happened nearly forty years ago! Kanak can no longer remember the face of the gentleman, although she recalls a few loving names he used to call her in their intimate moments together.

Kanakbala goes for a walk near the river with her dog, she sits on top of a rock to rest and to think of many old things as she stares at the dusty Shimul trees on the other side of the narrow river. The dog runs here and there and comes back at Kanak's feet and wags his tail. He looks up to his mistress in large glossy eyes to remind her of the happy days of the past. She wonders if the rich gentleman remembers their passion filled evenings—her gifts offered without any shame and reserve. She was not a young woman, even at age forty-one her body was as tight as a bow-string. After one special night of pleasure he brought her a gift—a puppy in a burlap bag. She named her Priya, the loved one. Priya one day grew up and in time gave birth to other puppies. Kanak kept one and gave away the rest to the fishmongers' wives in the market. Eventually, the little puppy grew old and limped around and one day disappeared like Kanak's gentleman who never returned.

Kanak found her current pet on the walk near the river. She gave him some food. He followed her to her hut and became her constant companion.

Last Friday when Kanakbala went for her daily walk with her dog, a sudden storm gathered from nowhere followed by gusty winds and heavy rains. The dog jumped out of her lap and ran away. In the mist of rain Kanak could not figure out which direction he had gone. Without a name she could not call after him. She became confused about where she was and blind-sighted Kanak walked into the river.

The next morning one of Kanak's neighbors looked for her in her hut but she was not there. Her neighbors and friends discussed the possibility that Kanak must have left for the city looking for her gentleman client, but they wondered how she would look for him without his name.

The Mystery on the Göta Canal

On the occasion of their third wedding anniversary, the 50-yr-old Thomas Wilson and his wife by second marriage, Julia, decided to travel to Sweden, the country of Julia's ancestors. The Wilsons lived in New York. After days of internet search, they discovered that they could make a journey in small renovated steamships across southern Sweden from Stockholm to Gothenburg, a distance of 189 kilometers on waterways of lakes, rivers and sea – all connected by a man-made canal called Göta (pronounced Yota) Canal. Though expensive, it'd be an apt anniversary present to his new wife, Thomas thought.

"I heard a lot about the Yota Canal from my father whose grandfather was one of the engineers when the canal was first constructed in 1868. Father talked about organizing a trip for us along its entire course but it never materialized," Julia said when she saw the map of Sweden on the desk in front of her husband.

"Really? In that case we have to make this trip. First, we need to find out if any of your relatives are still alive. Imagine meeting them on our way across the country! Won't you like that?" Thomas asked with enthusiasm.

"I have already made those queries. A cousin of my father's twice removed and his wife live in Gotland province in the middle of Sweden. I'm thinking of sending them an e-mail introducing myself and suggest a meeting if they are interested," Julia said eagerly.

"Great. Let me find a detailed map from the library tomorrow and we'll see if your cousins live anywhere near the Yota Canal. Perhaps they can meet us at the boat even. I shall also look into getting the tickets. So you go ahead and e-mail your cousin immediately. We have only a few weeks left to prepare everything," Thomas told his wife before leaving for the library.

"Why don't you use the Google map? Isn't that more precise and up-to-date?" Julia asked with a smile.

"You know me. I prefer the old-fashioned maps where I can find things with a simple magnifying glass. Perhaps, I'm more old-fashioned than I like to admit." Julia came close and planted a quick kiss on her husband's lips saying,

"I love you old-fashioned. Stay this way."

Two months after the above conversation, on a Wednesday morning of July, 2008, Thomas and Julia Wilson boarded the antique mahogany boat named Juno at the city pier of Skeppsbron in Stockholm. Juno (supposedly the world's oldest cruise ship) was built in 1874 in Sweden and still goes through the Göta Canal every summer carrying tourists. A charming boat of three floors, Juno can house around forty passengers including its ten crew members, several of whom are high school or college students of both sexes who are slim and of pale skin and long hair but quite muscular. Every summer students like these take the job to earn a few crowns and just to enjoy the sail in a quaint boat across the country for free. They mix freely with the passengers chatting, laughing and answering questions.

The first rays of the morning sun began to spread on the eastern sky, a few screeching sea gulls were flying low over the pier in search of breakfast. The passengers began to trickle in, in pairs or groups. The middle-aged captain of Juno, Peter Nostrom, with first officer Jan Jonson and a woman officer cum tour guide Viveca, stood at the head of the gangway welcoming the passengers to the boat. Passengers boarded Juno carrying two carry-on bags, the only luggage they were allowed on board.

One of the young crew picked up Julia's bag and asked them to follow him. Their cabin was one of the eight on the lower deck and was too small for two people to move around although it was well designed with several wall closets and a folding desk. A covered sink with hot and cold water stood on top of two drawers near the head of two bunk beds. They were asked to empty their bags and leave them in the corridor to be picked up and moved to storage. After Julia unpacked and put away their few pieces of clothing in the closets, they came up to the main deck to watch Juno leaving the dock.

Julia leaned against the railing and felt excited about the next four days when she would be on a dream trip with her beloved husband exploring this beautiful country from where her forefathers came. A few officegoers waved as they rushed toward their destinations in the city. Julia waved back happily feeling sorry for them because they had to work. Juno, in the meantime, spewed black smoke making a *bhok bhok* sound followed by a couple of horns and began to move away from the jetty. It passed the old brick buildings – the famous landmarks like the Opera House, House of the Nobility, the City Hall, The Nobel Museum. Leaving all these familiar landmarks behind, within a few minutes Juno entered the Baltic Sea – a span of shining slate black water strewn with thousands of islands of dark granite of various shapes and sizes. Some of the bigger ones had homes with red-tiled roofs surrounded by dark green trees; some had tiny rowboats tied near the water giving them an ambiance of a fairytale world. These were summer homes of the city dwellers.

"Are you Swedish? Do you know if there are ferry services between the mainland and these islands?" Thomas asked a tall gentleman who was standing near him watching the slowly receding city from their sight.

"Yes. There are several daily ferries that connect these islands to the mainland, only in the summer, of course. Most of the islands are connected by telephone and electric cables. By the way, I'm Lars Erikson; I live in Upsala and teach economics at the Upsala University." The middle-aged tall nice-looking gentleman extended his right hand toward Thomas to shake.

"I'm Thomas Wilson. My wife Julia's father's family is Swedish. We're taking this trip to see your beautiful country. We live in New York and I'm a civil engineer by profession," Thomas said as he shook Professor Erikson's stretched hand.

"Oh, you'll love this trip. This Yota Canal is a unique example of the excellence of Swedish civil engineering of the last century." Within a few minutes the two men began to chat on various topics and Thomas learned a lot of useful information about their boat trip from the knowledgeable professor. For example, the Göta Canal connects three rivers, eight lakes and a section of Baltic Sea. Meanwhile, Julia went downstairs to shower. A gong announced the coffee hour as the two men were about to discuss American foreign policy. They walked toward the dining room where Julia was waiting for Thomas. Professor Erikson tipped his hat with a smile toward her, excused himself and looked around for his wife. Thomas planted a quick kiss on his wife's lips.

They had their coffee and sweet buns with cardamom, a traditional coffee cake. The captain moved around greeting each table and requested they gather at the parlor of the main deck for orientation later. "I better go down and get my sweater, it's chilly here." Julia said as she kept rubbing her bare arms with both hands.

"I'll get it for you" Thomas said and rushed out of the dining room and in his hurry nearly bumped into a woman near the stairs.

"I'm so sorry," he said and looked at the woman with auburn hair that was moving with the ship's slight swing. Her bright brown eyes danced with a naughty smile as she looked at Thomas and said,

"I'm sorry too because you managed not to bump into me." As Thomas tried to find a suitable response to this daring flirtatious comment, she disappeared. By the time he got back to the dining room with Julia's sweater most of the passengers had already headed for the upstairs deck.

"What took you so long? Your coffee has become cold." Ignoring her comment, he gulped his cold coffee. As he looked around, he saw only one other table with two women and one of them was waving at him. Thomas recognized the pretty woman he almost bumped into earlier. Before he could wave back, the woman came over with her companion and introduced themselves. They were identical twins named Jill and Joan from Perth, Australia and were traveling around the world. Julia could not help noticing that Thomas's eyes rested on Jill's a bit longer.

At the orientation Captain Nostrom gave a brief history of Juno and pointed out various things on the ship and ended his speech by saying, "Although a historic journey, this is not an ocean voyage, therefore the possibility of a sudden natural disaster is minimal. However, when the ship passes through the two large lakes the wind direction may change to create some gust and turbulence. The biggest attraction of this trip is that in next four days we'll cross sixty-six locks! When the ship goes through the locks, the passengers are allowed to get off and get on board again on the other side. Such a crossing can take from twenty to thirty minutes."

The tour guide and second officer Viveca whispered something to the captain who nodded and added, "When you are on the land, you will have to listen to Viveca's instructions, and no one is allowed to go on their own. The ship will not wait for anyone who may get lost in the woods or in a town square shopping. Viveca will announce the time and place of separate shopping trips." The captain smiled and stopped. Then as if he just remembered something, he raised his right index finger and added, "The ship library is small, but it has some good books about the history of this canal and locks. Feel free to read them to familiarize yourselves with the route we're taking. Enjoy your stay with us and we hope you will come back again to take this historic trip with your friends and family. Any questions?" After waiting a couple of minutes, the captain climbed only ten steps to get back to his bridge.

Within a few minutes after the captain's speech, the gong rang to announce the lunch hour. The dining room hummed with conversations. Julia noticed that two tables out of eight were empty making the number of passengers only twenty-four. When she mentioned that to Thomas, he simply said, "Some people may be absent because they are not hungry." He looked around as if looking for some one. Julia already met a few people over coffee. Besides Thomas, herself, Professor Erikson and his wife Ulla, the Australian sisters, there were two middle-aged English couples, two Norwegian old ladies (who sat next to them at coffee break), a tall and muscular German and half a dozen University students who were doing research on the canal. A gay couple was always together and seemed very friendly.

After a delicious lunch of poached salmon with dill sauce and boiled new potatoes with butter and chive, watercress salad, followed by a fruity dessert, Julia and Thomas went to the upper deck to see the surrounding landscape. Passengers were scattered on the deck; a few men lay on the deck chairs smoking cigars, some leaned against the railing trying to take pictures. The distance between the shore and the slowly moving ship was so narrow that one could almost touch the trees and bushes on the shore. Julia's eyes and heart were full of new discoveries. She was tempted to climb the railing to try to touch the white smooth bark of the birch trees standing in long rows.

"Look, look Tom. So many wild chanterelle mushrooms under the leaves in between the birch trees, and also red lingonberries peeking through the fallen leaves. Oh, how I wish I could jump overboard and pick some!" Julia's enthusiasm touched Thomas. He smiled at his wife tenderly and said,

"Maybe you'll get a chance when we get off the boat to cross the locks tomorrow." Meanwhile the scenery of the shore changed from birch forest to farmland with golden wheat and barley of a dull green color. Julia had never seen any barley fields before. Wild straw flowers as blue as the eyes of Scandinavian girls scattered through the barley field making the field look like a huge bed spread with blue embroidery on it, Julia thought.

"Aren't the straw flowers beautiful? They seem to thrive in barley fields. By the way, I'm Ulla Erikson. Our husbands have already met this morning." After introducing herself, Julia shook Mrs. Erikson's hand happily.

"I'm so happy my husband had the idea to make this trip. I'm loving everything – the passengers, food, the beautiful landscapes of the shores." After a few minutes of chat, Julia excused herself and began to go downstairs to their cabin. The slow swing of the ship made her a bit sleepy. She looked around for Thomas but could not see him. On the port side of the main deck Julia saw one of the young crew members – a tall young man with a blond ponytail – laughing with a woman passenger, who was none other than one of the Australian twins. They did not pay any attention to Julia.

On the second morning the wind picked up. Despite the turbulence and rough ride, Julia was in a good mood because her Swedish cousin Theo and his wife Laili were due to come and meet them today when the ship would stop for the first lock. She had already called them with the exact location of Juno. This information was offered by Viveca. Julia dressed carefully in a cotton skirt and blouse set which had tiny red flowers on the fabric of light green. A red silk scarf around her neck matched the dress nicely. "You look beautiful this morning, darling." Thomas greeted her at the breakfast table with a kiss on her lips. When they went up to the main deck to watch the ship approach the lock, a sudden gust of wind stole Julia's expensive scarf. The first officer Jan Johnson was approaching at that very moment and saw what happened. He approached Julia and said kindly,

"If you're lucky your scarf may show up. Sometimes such pieces of material can be stuck at the bottom of the ship and we can retrieve them when the ship rises to the lock. It's also possible that the scarf will be returned by the same wind which may easily turn to another direction and drop it where it was picked up." He smiled at her sweetly before rushing to the bridge. Julia was pleased by the officer's words.

After breakfast that morning, Juno stopped for the first lock. All the passengers got off. The group of students borrowed bikes from the ship. With their back packs on their backs and cameras hanging around their necks off they went for their research. Since her cousin and his wife were due in half an hour, Julia decided to stay on board and watch how the lock goes up and down. Thomas went to the top deck with his binoculars, promising his wife to let her know as soon as he spotted her cousins. Julia was absorbed in the activities of the crew. A stout woman with a huge bunch of keys appeared from nowhere, climbing out of a Volvo to open the lock. Three young crew members got down on the lower deck and tried to balance the ship. The young man with the ponytail flashed his teeth at her and said,

"Please move away from the railing. It's not safe. If you want to take pictures the other corner may be a better spot." Julia mentioned the loss of her scarf partly to make a conversation. Unlike the first officer, the young crew member did not give her any hope of retrieving it. Julia looked down at the clear water below. Nothing could hide in this clear transparent water, Julia thought. Meanwhile one of the twin Australian sisters appeared and greeted Julia and joined her in watching the deft efficiency of the crew in balancing the ship as it went down in the lock chamber, before proceeding when the other side of the lock chamber was opened. She was fascinated by the quick movements of the young man's arm muscles as he maneuvered the operation of going through the lock rapidly. Occasionally he looked up to the Australian and exchanged a smile – perhaps one of the few fringe benefits of this hard summer job for the student, Julia told herself.

Thomas came down to tell her that he located two people biking toward the ship at a good distance. They had a big dog with them.

"Oh, they must be Laili and Theo. They did write me that their dog would come with them, and they would wear red jackets. Do they have red jackets on?" Julia was genuinely excited.

"Well, I haven't noticed the color of their jackets." Thomas said.

In fifteen minutes the Wilsons walked on the shore to receive their relatives. Julia never believed that their plan to meet like this would work! Laili brought a home-made cake called Tosca torta and a thermos full of strong Swedish coffee. Theo gave Julia a bunch of wild summer flowers. They sat under a tree near the canal and talked about their ancestors as they ate pieces of delicious cake. Julia felt as if she had known this couple all her life. They were simple, warm and sincere. Thomas spotted Viveca on board the ship gesturing for them to return. They had to say goodbye. Julia put on her sunglasses to hide her teary eyes. They hugged one another, promising to keep in touch. Theo and Laili waited with their dog another ten minutes and kept waving until Juno passed them by. Thomas left for the library and Julia ran to the stern, the last point of the ship and kept waving at her cousins until they became two red dots. She was sad and wanted to be alone and climbed to the top deck which was empty except for two figures who stood in an embrace near the flag post with a flapping Swedish flag. One of the figures must have heard her and turned back and Julia recognized Jill, one of the Australian sisters. Her companion was the big German man. "Excuse me," Julia said quickly and turned away from them and walked down the stairs.

After lunch the ship stopped again for another lock and the passengers got off walking along the canal on a narrow path to visit the town called Karlshamn, famous for making punch – a concoction of fruit juices and vodka that used to be consumed by the Swedes in ample quantity during the Christmas season. The towns like this along the canal are small, clean and sparsely populated with one street of half a dozen shops, a post office, sometimes a library, a square and a park. A handful of elderly people sat on the park benches and greeted the boat passengers. One old, retired navy-man came all dressed up in navy uniform carrying his accordion to the boat and sang navy songs – sung by drunken sailors – to entertain the passengers, who paid little attention. Julia felt sorry for the singer and dropped two crowns in his hat.

In the late afternoon Juno anchored near what used to be a military base. The passengers were led by an ex-army officer turned museum guide to the base, most of which was now a military museum. The old base was also used for the young recruits to practice target shooting when they fulfilled their one year of compulsory military training. The whole place was like an artificially set-up film studio with uniformed dummies holding real guns. The guide spoke in Swedish and English with a dose of humor making fun of Swedish military tradition. An ongoing video continued to present some Interactive Images of the past military activities. The passengers were led through a long dark and dusty tunnel with simulated intermittent gunshots to imitate the atmosphere of a battle field. An elderly Swedish man in his nineties - not a passenger of Juno - fainted in his wife's fragile arms - an event not known to any of the group until the wife's scream of distress was heard. The dark dusty tunnel with fake soldiers holding real guns was a bit much for the poor man's nerves. The guide acted quickly and carried him out of the tunnel filled with war sounds and the old man felt better when he breathed fresh air.

That evening Juno entered the big lake of Veteran. Immediately the wind became stronger as predicted by the captain the first day. The mood inside the ship also changed. Fewer people talked and still fewer laughed aloud. At dinner, wine and coffee spilled on several white tablecloths. One of the English couples commented that this old ship could not be pressurized to absorb the rough sail. That night Julia had hard time falling asleep maybe because of the turbulence. She suddenly remembered to tell Thomas about the intimate sight of the Australian sister and the big German on the top deck.

"Are you sure, the man was the big German?" Thomas asked from the upper bunk.

"Yes, I'm sure. Why is that so important?" Julia asked. No response came from the upper bunk this time. After a few minutes Julia thought Thomas must have fallen asleep.

The third day of the trip began with a cloudy sky, gusty wind along with cold misty rain as if the summer season had moved into autumn overnight. In the dining room everyone was dressed in sweaters or light parkas of various colors and the topic of conversation was invariably the weather. Some complained about sleeping poorly due to the loud sounds of the locks and the rough waters. Julia was not in the mood to join these talks. She greeted the Eriksons briefly and walked out to the deck which was not very pleasant because of the cold wind. She wondered where Thomas was. He had disappeared since breakfast. She needed to drink something warm and decided to look for a cup of hot tea. As she approached the kitchen she heard loud laughter and saw the gay couple chatting with the kitchen stuff. One of them welcomed Julia warmly and said,

"Come join us. We're finding out the latest ship gossip. Apparently last night someone saw one of the Australian sisters in a compromising position with a crew member. Right now, the crew member is being interrogated by the first officer." Julia showed little interest in the story and got out of the kitchen as soon as she got a cup of hot water and a tea bag. For a second she wondered if the sister in question was Jill or Joan. Julia went by the parlor and the library looking for her husband but could not locate him. She decided to go to their cabin and finish her tea there. To her surprise she found the door to their cabin locked from inside. Thomas must be taking a nap. He too had complained at breakfast about not sleeping well the night before. As she turned back to go upstairs she ran into one of the Australian sisters.

"Have you seen Jill? I can't find her anywhere." Joan sounded very worried.

"No, I haven't. Sorry. She may be sleeping in your cabin. Many people did not sleep well last night." As Julia uttered these words an idea popped in her head. She turned back down to their cabin again. This time the door was unlocked, and nobody was inside. Thomas's bed was exactly the same as it was earlier. She went up to the main deck but could not shake off a nagging surprise. Julia finally found her husband reading the newspaper in the parlor.

"Here you are! I have been looking for you everywhere." Julia sat down on the sofa next to Thomas with a sigh of relief.

"What are you talking about? How can I be lost in this tiny ship? You're such a worry wart!" Julia was shocked by his scolding tone. To make her husband's mood lighter she said,

"Is there any big news in the world?"

"What can happen in three days?" Thomas asked in annoyance. Before Julia could respond, Anna, the waitress in tight white skirt brought in morning coffee and cardamom buns. Everybody rushed inside from the chilly deck for hot coffee. Anna raised her voice to announce,

"This is our last evening, so you all are the captain's guests. Ladies, this is your chance to look your best, so do dress up. A lottery will decide which two ladies will sit at the captain's and first officer's table tonight. Good luck!"

At six in the evening the dinner began. Apart from the captain's table the rest of the passengers could sit at any table they wanted. Julia found herself next to the two Norwegian old ladies. She saw that Thomas was sitting between Jill and Joan at their table. For some unknown reason Julia lost her appetite for the six-course dinner. The menu began with wild mushroom soup followed by three kinds of pickled herring and venison with chanterelle sauce. The dessert had four different torts with ice-cream. She kept drinking tiny glasses of snaps throughout dinner. The captain stood up to give a brief speech ending with the lines, "This trip, our last this year, has been very smooth and uneventful. The only mentionable accident was the loss of Mrs. Wilson's beautiful scarf and no crew member can be blamed because Mother Nature arranged for the wind to do the little crime. Even the captain has no authority over the wind." Everyone laughed with the captain.

After dinner Thomas told Julia that he needed to go for a brisk walk on the top deck, he'd eaten too much. Julia was quite tipsy and sleepy from all the snaps she swallowed, so she told him that she'd go to bed. On her bed there was a computer printout with an instruction that the passengers must pack their bags (which are in front of their cabins) by early the next morning and leave them in front of their cabins to be picked up. The ship was to reach the destination, Gothenburg, the next day. Julia was too tired to pack. She needed to go to bed. Her mood did not improve even after downing all the alcohol. By the third day the excitement of the first two days had paled considerably. The only highlight was meeting with her long-lost cousins. With this last thought she fell into a deep sleep. She had no idea if or when Thomas came to the cabin that night.

On the fourth or the last day of the canal trip, the ship was buzzing with activities. Some of the crew members were busy gathering the luggage of the passengers on a corner of the main deck, others were busy covering up ropes, cables and other loose tools with heavy plastics. The young crewman with the ponytail was busy washing the upper deck with a big hose. They were served a skimpy breakfast. Julia climbed to the top deck to take some pictures before Juno entered the industrial outskirts of Gothenburg, their destination. One of the Australian sisters – after four days together, Julia still could not figure out if it was Jill or Joan – stood on one end of the deck. "Good morning!" Julia greeted her. She then added, "How is your sister?"

"Good morning! My sister? I really do not know. I haven't seen her since dinner last evening. She may have gone to bed late when I was already asleep. This morning she must have gotten up very early and left the cabin for some adventure or whatever. I cannot keep an eye on her twenty-four hours a day. She's always been the wild one in the family." Joan stopped with a smile. However, Julia did not find any reason to smile at her statement at all. She could not help remembering a few snippets of images – loud laughter with the young crew, the kitchen gossip about her and the intimate embrace with the big German – etc. etc. She simply said,

"Your sister could not possibly be lost in such a small ship. Perhaps she is chatting with the captain in his bridge and learning about sailing an old ship like this."

"I doubt that. Anyway, thanks."

By now Juno had left the charming rural nature and entered the suburb of a city spotted with tall white chimneys of various factories and high-rise buildings. Julia felt a jolt as if suddenly a nice melody was interrupted. The four days of relaxed stress-free simple life on board the renovated old ship was about to end. The sadness of losing something she never knew hit her. She closed her camera and looked back to the disappearing landscape. Her husband appeared from nowhere and touched her back gently. As she turned in surprise, he kissed her right cheek and said,

"Let's go to the bow of the ship. I want to watch the ship enter the mouth of the Gothenburg harbor. Thank God, we finally can leave this ship – a veritable can of sardines! Finally, I can spread out." He began to walk toward the bow rapidly without waiting for her. Julia was shocked and hurt by his words, the way he talked about the trip – something they lovingly planned together. She followed him to the other side of the ship and saw a small crowd. Everyone was bending down on the railing to see something and talking in excitement. She saw Ulla Erikson from a distance. Before she could talk to Mrs. Erikson, Thomas who was ahead of her suddenly grabbed her arm and led her back to the direction they came from.

"What's the matter? Let me go, you're hurting me! What are the people looking at?" Julia screamed at her husband. The ship came to a sudden halt. The captain's voice came through the intercom,

"We just landed at Gothenburg. Unfortunately, we cannot disembark yet. Because of an unforeseen accident, we all have to stay on board at least for next ten to twelve hours. Please do not step out of the ship. The local police will begin an investigation immediately. Everyone should move to the parlor. The kitchen crew will get some sandwiches shortly. I'm awfully sorry for this inconvenience. Please wait for further instructions." He stopped without any niceties. Julia looked at Thomas and asked without sound,

"What's the matter?" Thomas was looking away. Mrs. Erikson came forward from the disoriented crowd and led Julia to a corner and whispered,

"Doesn't that scarf belong to you? I recognized it. You wore it the other morning."

"What are you talking about? I don't follow a single word of what you said." Julia sounded desperate and totally confused. She looked for Thomas but could not locate him. Ulla Erickson said,

"This morning when Juno was about to enter the harbor, it stalled. The first officer and the captain came down from the bridge and noticed that something was stuck to the bottom of the ship and prevented its movement. The stuck object was a woman's body. A few passengers were already on the deck and the news spread like fire. The captain ordered a couple of young crew members to recover the body. I happened to be doing my morning walk and saw two young men carrying a covered body. A scarf just like the one you wore hung out of the covered body. Later I heard that it was Jill, one of the Australian twins. The other sister is at the captain's office right now." Mrs. Erikson stopped to take a long breath, which sounded like a sigh. Julia dropped herself on a deck chair. Many thoughts and snippets of memories came crowding in her head. She could not be sure what to think. The shock of the news made her numb. The only thing she wanted right now was Thomas's reassuring touch. She wanted to hold his hand tight. But he was nowhere to be seen. She looked at Mrs. Erikson and asked in teary voice,

"Have you seen my husband?" At that moment the captain's voice came through the speaker again. He announced the arrival of a coroner and the detectives from the city's police department. He urged the passengers to gather in the parlor immediately.

The police investigation continued for three days. Everyone was interrogated for hours. On the morning of the second day the Eriksons, the Norwegian old ladies, one of the English couples, the gay couple and the group of students all were allowed to disembark. Ulla Erikson hugged Julia tenderly before leaving and whispered in her ears, "Good luck my dear!" Then on the third day Julia, Thomas and the rest of the passengers were allowed to leave as well. Apparently, the police found nothing definite and concluded that Jill perhaps committed suicide or accidentally fell into the water and hit her head against the ship's bow.

The Wilsons took a suite in a luxury hotel in Gothenburg for a few days before going back to New York. The reservation had been made before they left the States. Julia had not exchanged any words with her husband since they had left the ship. She drew a hot bath in the spacious bathroom, undressed and went inside the foamy warm water. She closed her eyes and hoped to wash away all her confusions, doubts and questions. It seemed like a long time back when she was so happy with the beauty of the canal and the passing landscapes and her meeting with her new relatives. That happiness is now buried under sadness, anxiety and mistrust. After the bath she would ask her husband a few questions. She was no longer sure he'd answer truthfully.

Illegal Immigrant

Morena Abanibe, in an old parka and a hand-made woolen cap, walks toward Harvard Square where she'll take bus no. 77 to Watertown, and then another bus to visit her brother in a penitentiary. It's early April and the last touch of late winter lingers in the air. The sidewalks of Green Street, behind Central Square where she lives, have tiny mounds of snow which cover the wobbly stems of already bloomed crocuses. After nearly thirty years in this country, Morena still marvels at these tiny beautiful flowers coming out of cold snow. In Nigeria where she grew up, flowers bloom only in hot sun.

She came to America to be with her baby brother who came to this continent at age twenty as an illegal immigrant. He managed to survive ten years by cleaning people's homes, and finally owned his own cleaning business. One day he wrote his older sister an urgent letter saying how he missed his favorite food, *jollof* rice, that Morena cooked for him when he was a little boy. "Please come for a visit, he said. "You can stay with me. I'm sending your airfare with a friend." Morena was overjoyed with the prospect of a reunion with her only sibling and with the help of an American missionary, she obtained a plane ticket and tourist visa. That was in 1974.

A lot of water has flowed through the Charles River since. Morena was lucky to find a job as a housekeeper with a wealthy white family—a childless kind couple in Cambridge. They have employed her all these years and let her stay in a studio above their garage on Cottage Street. When she had enough savings to return to her homeland, she had no family left to go back to. So she remained with the people who were not family and grew old. She had a few men friends when she first came but no one was special enough to start a life together. She has made a few women friends at the local Senior Center with whom she goes shopping. But even after all these years, she does not feel at home in this city of cold winters and strange people who never laugh aloud.

Her brother hasn't done so well. He got involved with the wrong kind of people and got into drugs, mostly selling. He has been incarcerated several times, and he is finally serving a sentence of life imprisonment without parole for fatally shooting a gang member. Her brother's widow, an African American woman, shed no tears and left with their two sons without a forwarding address. Morena often wondered if those kids took their father's name, Abanibe, an honorable tribal name, they should be proud of.

On her walk this morning, as she looks up from the little garden where the crocuses finished blooming, she sees a big bird like a pheasant crossing the street. She nearly jumps in sudden shock of joy seeing something that looks like a bird of her childhood. She cannot imagine a bird walking on Green Street of Cambridge that looks like a wild pheasant. She decides it must be a wild turkey. Or could it be that she is seeing things! At her age anything is possible. The next minute the bird disappears through an alley between two houses leaving a trace of old country memory. Morena is happy that she can share the story of the bird with her brother. Otherwise they will sit silently for an hour after he eats all the *jollof* rice she brings for him. Morena's old eyes fill up with tears as she watches him eat the rice eagerly—his childhood food from his home in Nigeria.

A Wedding Gift

"Attention, attention, due to political disturbances at the border all trains to Bangladesh are cancelled indefinitely. All trains..." The loudspeaker blurted out again and again as Anita Bose and her husband waited at the main railway station in Kolkata, beyond the scheduled time for the train to arrive. Mrs. Bose looked at her husband briefly without a word. She dropped herself on the dirty platform, ruining her clean starched sari. As she sobbed, Mr. Bose looked down at his wife. She was fifty-eight years old. But he saw a little girl who had just lost all the toys she possessed.

Mr. Bose hesitated two full minutes before stretching his hands to touch her slightly trembling shoulders. She controlled herself, wiped her tears and stood up using his outstretched hand as support. Without a word they walked toward the exit of the platform to return home, the same home from which she so desperately had to escape only an hour before.

It all happened three weeks back when Mrs. Bose decided to dust the bookshelves in the living room herself – a chore usually done by one of the maids. As she climbed up on a stool to dust the high shelf, she saw the leather-bound volume that her tutor had given her as a wedding gift years ago. She took the volume out, dusted it carefully and opened it. The tutor's handwriting was still fresh on the page next to the cover with his signature on the second line. It read:

Wish you a most prosperous and happy future!
Affectionately, Sunil Das

She leafed through the pages and a smell of her youth hit her. She sat on the stool, holding the book, reading at places, and the old memories trickled back to her slowly and gradually. How eagerly she waited for those afternoons once a week. Her tutor came to discuss what she had read, chapters he'd selected the week before. These were books on classical literature – translations from Sanskrit scholars, the poet Kalidasa in particular.

Anita's librarian father wanted his daughter to be educated as much as possible since she could not go to the college in their small town because it was meant for men only. The private tutor, Mr. Das, who was a professor at that college, agreed to help her in reading some philosophy and literature. Sometimes her father joined them in the discussion when her mother served tea and homemade sweets. Anita was a teenager, only 17 years old.

She liked to read again and again the heart-wrenching story of Shakuntala, a hermit's adopted daughter who lost her beloved prince because he had forgotten their chance encounter. The heroine of the story pined away in her sorrow of rejection. Anita lay on her bed in the long summer afternoons reading how even the cool lotus leaves could not soothe the scorching body of the lovelorn maiden of the book. Somehow the love story made her own hot bed more tolerable. Afterwards, during the rainy season, she lost herself in the pages of *Megha Duta* where the imprisoned lover composed exquisite lyrics and begged the monsoon clouds to carry them to his ladylove far, far away. A gathering storm outside Anita's window made the lyrics extremely believable. How impatiently she waited to discuss those classics with her tutor from every point of view – style, grammar, syntax, all. It seemed like wandering through the forests and cities of the past with the tutor by her side ready for adventure of love and painful loss. Then the time really came to make the journey.

One Sunday morning as she was passing her parents' room she overheard her mother saying,

"How about thinking of finding a marriage proposal for our daughter? Are you listening to me?"

"Um.... Yes, what were you saying? What happened? What's the hurry? She is only 17. She is so interested in her studies right now." Obviously, her father was reading the Sunday newspaper.

"So, you think! She is interested in her studies, really? Haven't you noticed how carefully she dresses every time…? But then you never notice anything anyway." After a sigh, "If you don't do anything, I will - before it's too late. You don't want to see your daughter suffer the rest of her life in poverty as a professor's wife, do you?"

Anita ran from the hallway, climbing the steps up to the roof terrace where she would be alone. She did not wish to hear any more. The word marriage nearly burned her ears with unknown pleasures and dreams. She was to be married! Married! Married to whom? Someone like the prince in the story?

The next six months passed rapidly. She continued to meet her tutor for her weekly lessons, but became quite preoccupied with her own dreams. Then the day finally arrived. One spring evening she was married to Mr. Bose who was eleven and a half years older and came from seven hundred miles away. She remembered that day very well. It was a clear day in February in the middle of spring season in Bengal, full of noises, relatives and guests. There were the fragrances of jasmines and tube roses and also the aroma of food. She felt very special, like the heroines in her favorite classics. She also felt nervous about the unknown future as she packed her trunk with the wedding gifts, including the one from her tutor. She noticed how Professor Das swallowed hard when he handed her the leather-bound volume of the collected works by the Sanskrit poet they both loved.

All this happened in the past – so far back in the past – it seemed like another life. Anita Bose kept all that away in distant memory, just as she kept the leather-bound volume, the only wedding gift that still existed, on the high shelf beyond her reach. She never had time or desire to open that book. Her mother and relatives were wise. She had been married to a kind and responsible man, who had never given her economic hardship or any other kinds of problems. At fifty-eight she was a content wife and mother. Her children were settled, boys holding good jobs, daughters were married and healthy. Yes, she had been fortunate.

A prosperous married life indeed! The other thought that followed as she still held the volume of Sanskrit poetry, revealed another truth. She had not lived what she dreamed of – not even a small fraction of it. She could not recall one occasion in all these years when she had lost her head or her heart, either in pleasure or in pain. Yes, she had been fortunate, but not happy. What would she not do to go back to only one of those afternoons when she was seventeen! Oh, if only she could ever feel anything like that again! How eagerly she had wanted to be married, without realizing that her marriage closed the door forever to what it promised, and opened another to a comfortable life that she now began to question.

Anita Bose spent the rest of the day feeling restless. As the days came and went, she began to feel as if she were awakened from a long sleep induced by a sedative, a sleep so deep that she could not recall even a fleeting dream. She knew now that she must do something but could not be sure what. All of a sudden, she was lost in her familiar surroundings. She noticed that she had lost her appetite and could not read her favorite magazines before her afternoon nap. She began to avoid her neighbors and friends. Gossip over tea lost its attraction. One morning she lingered in bed long after her habitual hour of rising. The next day she was up at dawn and found nothing to do. That evening she looked into the tall mirror as she combed her long hair into a loose bun. Her hand shook as she saw the face of a stranger that looked back at her.

Soon her restlessness increased manifold, as if time was running out. But what was it that she expected from her marriage? No, it was not just the romance her tutor kindled in her heart years ago. She knew now that it had to do with an intensity – a height and a depth. She did not even know if her husband or her family had anything to do with it. She was afraid to ask herself if she had lived at all. This nagging feeling of being betrayed drove her to a desperation that she could not shake off. The worst of all was the unanswered question 'who betrayed her?' She had no choice but to act.

So, one evening, nearly a month after that fateful day when she dusted the bookshelves, Anita Bose approached her husband. Mr. Bose spent a lot of time reading religious books since his retirement five years back. She told him that she would like to go away for a while.

"Why not?" he casually said, "Where would you like to go? Should I write to one of the daughters? We could go and visit Mira. It would be nice to see your favorite granddaughter. She must be quite grown by now. I wouldn't mind a break from this city, myself." Mrs. Bose surprised her husband when she said,

"No, I don't want to visit anyone. I want to go away alone, by myself, somewhere. Please allow me. I shall make arrangements for the servants to look after you. I want to go away, maybe for one month or more."

Mr. Bose shut his book, looked at her and asked, "Are you alright?"

"Yes, yes, I am fine. No, I am not so fine. I don't know how I feel. Please, please let me go away for awhile."

Although puzzled by such an unusual request, her husband helped her to make the necessary arrangements to go to her hometown, which was now in Bangladesh. Once she obtained her passport and visa, Anita Bose sat down to pack her suitcase. She remembered the excitement and trepidation of forty years back when she had packed her trunks to join her husband. This time, however, she did not have any particular goal. She had a few distant cousins scattered near the town where she grew up and whom she knew well. She would find them. She knew the country and spoke the dialect. She would manage.

Then the day of her departure came and the train did not arrive to take her back to her small town where she grew up and where her private tutor taught her how to dream.

On the taxi returning home she sat quietly, her face turned away. Her husband looked at her out of the corner of his eye and pressed her palm slightly. He cleared his throat before saying, "How about taking a trip to the mountains with me? We can both get away for awhile. What do you say?"

She did not turn around to look at him, only burst out sobbing again as she held his hand tightly in hers.

Returning Home

The British Airways jet circled over Kolkata airport a few times before diving through the thick fog of January to descend on the tarmac.

"We just landed at Subhas Chandra International Airport of Kolkata. Please remain seated..." The usual announcement floated over the passengers who were bustling around getting ready to get off at their destination after twenty odd hours of flight for the majority of the passengers.

"Look, look Rita, the coco-palms around the city are still the same – standing erect to welcome us." Sujit looked out the window as he told his wife in a childlike glee. Rita was about to fix her hair and treat her face with a light touch of makeup looking at her tiny hand mirror. Without moving her gaze from the mirror, she simply said,

"Is that so? Let's see how the people of the city welcome us!" Sujit ignored the slight sarcasm in her words and kept looking out at the rapidly increasing size of the vegetation and houses as the plane kept descending. He could not help noticing the same kind of excitement he experienced every time he visited his birthplace during his thirty years of voluntary exile in America. Apart from the anticipation of meeting old school friends and tasting his favorite dishes prepared by his aunts and sisters-in-law, there is another kind of joy that hits him the moment he arrives in his country. This ineffable joy must have been hidden in every cell of his body and soul and becomes conscious when he lays eyes on the familiar land. Is this the proverbial "pull of the umbilical cord" that is realized only when one lives in another land, Sujit wondered?

On the other side of a railing barrier of the "baggage claim" Sujit's older brother Ajit stood smiling and waving at them. The moment they rolled up with the carriage full of three huge suitcases, Ajit grabbed his brother in a bear hug while Rita lowered herself to take the dust of his feet and touch her forehead in respect. Ajit immediately let go of Sujit and raised his younger sister-in-law with his two hands saying, "Live a long life Rita. You look beautiful. American climate must suit you well." Rita smiled demurely. Ajit's driver came forward, greeted the new guests and walked to the parking lot pushing the luggage cart and loaded the Maruti station wagon. Sujit was tireless and curious even after a flight of twenty-one hours and kept asking about everything as the car continued the thirty-mile road toward Kolkata city.

"How long do you plan to stay this time?" Ajit asked Rita and before she responded he added, "Every time you two come for a visit you never stay more than a month. Is it worth the cost and strain of the long flight?"

"As I already told you on the phone, I took an early retirement from my job on my 62nd birthday this year with the intention of returning home. Rita's keeping her teaching job at the college still. She has a sabbatical this year, therefore she has a year's break. She can retire later if we really decide to stay here permanently. At least that's the plan." Sujit said with a smile.

"Is that right? I'm very pleased to hear this. Excellent plan! In fact, you can begin the renovation of the house on Tilak Road which Father left for you and Rita. If you two settle in this country then my wife and I will be the first to welcome you. At our advancing age it's a relief to know that my only brother is living in the same neighborhood." The car just turned into the narrow lane where Ajit and his wife Neela lived in a two-storey building, so the conversation stopped for now.

A few days later when Sujit and Rita overcame their jet lag, the two brothers and their wives sat on their back veranda one afternoon having tea and snacks served by the maid. Sujit just had a sip of the tasty Darjeeling tea and a bite of home-made *samosa* and said to his sister-in-law, "Ah, what pleasure to have this high tea with you Boudi! Everything tastes so good in Kolkata."

"Now that you're here you can enjoy all the good food. Tell me, do you think you can really adjust back to this life and hot weather after so many years abroad? I hear no one wants to return after they live in America!" His sister-in-law said and looked at both Sujit and Rita. This time Rita responded.

"To tell you the truth I was not that keen on this plan. But Sujit has been talking about returning home ever since we got there. He really misses this city and his family. I like living in America. Also, our son is there, I don't know if I can live ten thousand miles away from him, no matter he's now a grown young man. I'm willing to give it a try and if things do not work out, we can go back. At least I'll have my job still."

"What does Rupak say about his parents' desire to move back to India?" Ajit asked Rita.

"He agrees with his father. He thinks we'll be happier here and aging will be easier among close relatives. He's twenty-five and sooner or later will have his own family. By the way, we haven't had a chance to tell you that Rupak has a promising offer from Google in California. If he accepts that offer, he can even travel to India on job and visit us occasionally."

"Not a single week of all these thirty years passed when I did not dream of returning. To tell you the truth I never put my roots down in that country," Sujit rejoined quickly. "Yes, I like working there and there are many amenities, but it's not my country with all my memories. My social security pension will expand more than seventy times in Indian currency. If Rita's pension is added, we can live here like royals." Sujit paused with a broad smile.

"Splendid! I'm all for your coming back. As soon as you're ready, let's have a look at the house on Tilak Road and you two can discuss a plan of renovation. It's important that you have a home you'd like to settle in. The Tilak Road house is old and in disrepair. It'll need extensive work. Neela had a kindergarten school in that house for about ten years before she retired from that hobby. So, it's all empty and ready for you to renovate," Ajit said with enthusiasm.

"Let's go and have a look right now." Sujit looked at his wife.

Within a week after this conversation Sujit interviewed several prospective construction companies along with a couple of well-known architects. After the blueprint of a total renovation was approved by Rita, Sujit signed a contract with one contractor, Mr. Dadra, who scribbled his name on the bottom line of the contract and flicked the butt of his cigarette outside the window. Flashing a row of yellow teeth he said, "I'm putting orders for the materials right away and will call you as soon as the suppliers ship them. I reckon we can begin the job in a couple of weeks, maybe three, tops."

"Good. I shall wait for your call, Mr. Dadra," Sujit said, not sure if he should shake his hand or not. He had forgotten the customs and conventions of this land. Mr. Dadra joined his palms briefly in a gesture of greetings, Indian style and left.

Over the next month or more Sujit used Ajit's car and driver, visiting various relatives and old friends with a square cardboard box of sweets in his hand for each family. He wanted to drive himself, but the traffic situation prevented him. Also, he needed practice in driving on the left side of the road. His friends and relatives were all very happy to see him. His second cousin by marriage, Tinki, invited him to stay for lunch and served him a dish with wide white beans with a purple border – something Sujit used to love and had not tasted for over thirty years!

"These beans still exist! How wonderful! You made my day Tinki-di. Wait till I tell Rita about this. She won't believe me. This is one of the reasons I returned home." Sujit was effusive.

"It's a pleasure to see how happy you are with such a small thing. You're lucky. These beans are not always available. They appear occasionally in the winter months," Tinki said.

Sujit concentrated in delighting himself in rediscovering the city – its sights and sounds. His meetings with some of his old friends did not go too well, however. After retirement several of them were away visiting their children in other cities. A number of them were suffering from chronic diseases like arthritis, hypertension and diabetes. They kept talking about their hopeless prognosis, corruption in every sphere of Indian life and increasing atmospheric pollution. Sujit remained depressed for several days after such visits. He did not like to be pulled down by people's negative attitudes. He was careful not to talk about it with his wife or brother and tried to distract himself making new notes about the renovation.

Meanwhile the contractor failed to call back even after six weeks. Sujit tried to reach him at his mobile without success until one day he got a response. The telephone conversation went like this:

"Hello, Mr. Dadra? You never called back. What's up? When do you start? Have you received the materials? If you're too busy tell me, I can always find other contractors." Sujit did not bother to hide his annoyance.

"Hello, sir, how are you? I hope your jet lag is over by now. No need to get anxious. I put in an order for the best Burmese teak wood and Rajathani marble. They need time to reach Kolkata. Also a few of my people got sick with malaria… the time of the year, you know. You're on top of my list. As soon as the materials arrive, I shall call you and begin the job. I give my word."

"Tell me when. Give me a date, not your word. Otherwise, I go to someone else." Sujit snapped.

"Please do not excite yourself, sir. Not good for your blood pressure. Okay, I promise to begin on the auspicious day next month after the new moon." The contractor said.

"What does the new moon have to do with the beginning of the construction?" Sujit was now really angry.

"In a big job such as this - remodeling your ancestral home - we need to be careful and choose a date which is blessed by the cosmic powers. We cannot afford to anger the god of construction and renovation, you know. As a matter of fact, I plan to do a *puja* to appease god Biswakarma before we begin. Do you think you can give me some advance..." Mr. Dadra said unfazed.

"I don't care which god you want to please or appease. I need a definite date from you right now." Sujit persisted.

"Sir, please don't be so impatient. In this country we don't have any control over any situation. If the gods are happy perhaps things will work out to our benefit. For example, the trucks or the train carrying your timber may not be stopped and looted by the border rebels like Naxalites if god Biswakarma is pleased with us. Therefore, I'm saying that we need to do a *puja* to ..."

"How about my firing you right now? I do not need your services anymore. I have a row of contractors waiting in line."

"Please, please sir. Don't be so rush. Okay I shall begin day after tomorrow. We can begin the demolishing part without the supply." Mr. Dadra said.

"I want to see you and your people at the Tilak Road address at 8 AM day after tomorrow. Otherwise, I employ another company." Sujit shut his mobile before Mr. Dadra could say anything more.

That evening at the dinner table when Sujit summarized his telephone conversation with the contractor to his older brother and sister-in-law, Ajit laughed and said,

"This is Kolkata, India not Rochester, New York. You will need infinite patience to get anything done in this city. If he does not show up, I will find a new contractor, don't worry. You also need to look at time differently." Ajit did not bother to elaborate on his last statement.

The renovation did begin that week and Sujit became a diligent supervisor and began to spend most of the day everyday at the old house. He told his wife, "This may be a good time for you to go visit your parents in Delhi. I'm too busy and there isn't anything for you to do right now. You may make some notes about the kind of furniture you want for different rooms. Be careful when you're there. Don't eat all those street foods that you like so much. I shall call you every other day with the progress." Rita, who had already approved the plan for a modern kitchen, agreed reluctantly to make the trip.

Sujit's occasional irritation with the work crew continued. The lame excuses when they came late, the way they disposed of the trash despite his hiring a dumpster and many more small things irked him. He also noticed that his brother and sister-in-law changed the topic when he complained too much about things. The other day a dead carcass of a dog on top of the heap of garbage at the crossing of Tilak and Lansdowne Road stank up the whole area and no one bothered to do anything. He called the municipality without any avail. When Sujit told his sister-in-law the story she finished her tea quickly without a comment and left the room with some small excuse. Sujit shrugged his shoulders and called his wife in Delhi and repeated the story. To his surprise Rita reacted by saying,

"You cannot change people's habits in this country. Try to ignore small things if you can. By the way, I may stay a bit longer; my second cousin etc. etc." Sujit realized that even his closest ally, his wife was in another world right now. He began to feel lonely and remembered their home in Rochester. Snippets of images came floating to his memory. In the long winter season when he awoke early and came downstairs to the kitchen and made coffee before going to work, the juniper bushes in front of the house stood in the grey dawn light like trusting guards protecting his home and the family. Sujit closed his eyes to recapitulate the image and the feeling of security but failed. A number of crows in the yard kept making a racket over a piece of food and the March sun was already beating down the earth with rapidly rising heat. It was impossible to go back to the cool moment of a winter morning in Rochester amid this noisy heat of the bright sun in Kolkata. Was it only the heat that was pushing him to go back to that memory? He wondered.

When Sujit called his wife in Delhi the next day, he told her how much he missed her. There was no one who understood him as she did, and he asked her to come back sooner than later. He also reported that, despite everything, he was pleased with the progress of the renovation which was going well after a sluggish start. All the doors and windows were changed with the latest model of double pane glass. The big roof terrace was totally rebuilt with a gentle slope for proper drainage during the monsoon.

Sujit asked Mr. Dadra to add a stone ledge to raise the sunniest part of the terrace for gardening. Rita might want to build a potted garden of fragrant summer flowers. He remembered an incident when they went to America thirty years ago soon after they were married. They arrived in Rochester in the spring of 1980, where they saw thousands of lilac bushes in bloom in a park and the scent of the lilac permeated the city air. Sujit picked a cluster of the lavender blossoms and gave them to his new bride. She was delighted but also worried that her husband could be arrested for stealing flowers from a public park. She immediately hid the flowers inside her handbag.

Sujit recognized the old but healthy tree *of Kadam* flower that was there since his childhood and now grew tall enough to almost touch the northeast corner of the roof of this three-storey home. The white-green round flowers bloomed during the rainy season. His mother wanted a few to worship the god Krishna who supposedly liked only *Kadam* flower. Sujit tied a small knife at the end of a broom stick and standing on the roof picked one or two clusters for his mother. She always told him, "Lord Krishna will bless you!" This memory of some fifty years back made his eye-lids moist. He cautioned the contractor's crew to be mindful not to cut down the *Kadam* tree even if it looked awkward where it was. Sujit was surprised to realize how much of his childhood and youth were still hidden in the old bricks and mortar of this two-hundred-year-old house. However, such attacks of nostalgia lasted only a brief time.

The renovation was finally over after exactly eleven months. Everything looked beautiful, from the polished marbles of the bathroom floors to the balconies attached to the three bedrooms facing south. Rita was very pleased with the renovation as well, although she noted that the budget far exceeded the original estimate. They justified it by saying to each other that the excellent workmanship was worth the extra fifty thousand dollars. Sujit and Rita invited all their relatives and many friends to a lavish house-warming party and proudly gave tours of their new home to the guests. Sujit slept soundly that night. His thirty years' dream of coming home finally was a reality. They settled down with a new car, a driver and two domestic servants.

With Ajit's help, Sujit began to get calls and offers for consulting jobs. Rita had sent in her resignation from her teaching position at the Community College in Rochester where she used to teach. She now applied for a teaching position at a local college. Even their son Rupak managed to come for a week to see them and their new home. Neither Sujit nor Rita expected such a smooth transition from Rochester to Kolkata.

One afternoon a couple of months after their house-warming party, Rita and her sister-in-law went shopping for gifts for a few friends and children for Christmas. Sujit was home alone. The cook prepared his afternoon tea with his favorite snacks and laid everything out on the balcony of the second floor. The weather even in December had not changed much. It was a hot day with occasional dry air from nowhere. Sujit took the cup of tea and decided to go up to the roof terrace hoping for a bit of southern breeze that was supposed to blow at this time of the day from the Bay of Bengal. He put his teacup on the ledge of the roof and looked around.

The high-rise buildings in the neighborhood obstructed his view, though he could hear the traffic noise below and from some distances away. He looked down and saw countless pedestrians – all rushing in all directions in the midst of streetcars, buses, cars, bicycles and three wheelers. The sun had set half an hour earlier; the dusk was yet to fall. The winter sky was hazy with smoke or smog showing only a dull pink brush stroke on the west. A row of swallows came and sat on the electric wire between his house and the neighbor's. On the top branches of the *Kadam* tree a flock of *Shalik* birds took shelter, perhaps for the night, making a cacophony of calls. The business of the day's end mingled with an impending disquiet of the early evening. Sujit became unmindful and lost his bearings. He silently uttered to himself,

"What am I doing here? I no longer belong to this house, this city, this country. I have known these birds and their calls since childhood and I'm familiar with the crowd of the streets below. But I am not one of them. I do not fit in..." He continued to brood about all the money he'd spent in renovating this ancestral home into a perfect modern house to live in. Everybody including his wife loved it. But... but something was missing.

Sujit stepped down from the roof terrace slowly. The empty teacup was forgotten. He was wrapped in a vague depression. That night in bed Sujit laid on their bed next to his wife and spoke slowly, "I think I need to call Dr. Sarkar tomorrow. I don't feel well."

"Why? What happened?" Rita turned immediately toward her husband in concern and touched his forehead to check if he had fever.

"I don't have fever, if that's what you're worried about." He turned back toward her and said, "I've no idea why I'm feeling so low. I'm afraid I've made a major blunder. I do not know why I feel I have no right to be here. I do not belong here anymore."

"What are you saying? For thirty odd years you repeated the mantra of returning home. We have spent nearly all our savings to renovate this house and now you think you made a mistake! When everything is within our reach,.. you think..."

His wife was too upset to finish her sentence. She got out of bed, pulled out several tissue papers from a box and began to cry loudly. Sujit came close to her, tried to put his arm around her and said,

"I cannot blame you for being angry with me. I don't understand it myself. You know very well that I'm not happy in America either. But I didn't realize that, inadvertently, that's the land where I put down roots. Coming back to India was a fantasy, nothing more."

Rita wiped her eyes and stared at her husband of thirty-five years in total disbelief.

Family

Looking for my Father

I already knew it. I have been keeping track of all the stops and the schedule for the last ten hours. We are only twelve minutes late. "Denver, Colorado. Seven minutes stop." The bus driver announces through his microphone.

I pick up my backpack from the overhead rack and maneuver my way down the aisle. The old man in front of me, who was snoring a minute ago, is now awake and yawns loudly. Two young people are cuddled up in their parkas – necks, arms and legs intertwined. Still, they look lonely like the rest of us in the bus. Outside, it begins to snow in tiny flakes and the bus station looks desolate in the dim lights. Two black women get off before me. The driver, who is unloading their luggage from the belly of the bus, looks up and asks, "Any bags for you sir?"

"Nothing for me, thanks." I swing my heavy backpack over my shoulder. This backpack was a gift from my brother five years ago on my nineteenth birthday and I like to carry it everywhere. I walk toward the door of the lobby. It feels good to reach my destination at last. It has been a long journey from home in Germany. The driver gets back in the bus and it begins to move. No new passengers at this hour.

Inside the lobby, I look around briefly. Would my father really come? It's not too late; a little after ten. Had he received my letter? He must have. I had written two months ago with a return address. I should have telephoned him from New York. But I could not bring myself to go that far. Right now, I have to use the toilet. The one inside the bus was so small and unstable that I could hardly stand straight. The stink did not bother me that much, although it was pretty bad. I have been to worse places.

The greyhound bus station toilet is a hotel room compared to that. In the toilet I see an elderly man using the nearest urinal. He has wispy gray hair and loose skin on his neck. He's hunched forward. He may be the same age as my father. I wait for him to finish and go near the sink. As I wash my face and look up to the mirror, I see his face behind me. I watch as he opens his fly and makes a few unmistakable gestures. I feel hollow inside my gut. I turn around and almost run to the door. Damn. I needed to pee so bad.

Sexual overtures must be the same all over the world. The Navy man who walked up to me in the woods by the fairground near Frankfurt one summer made the same gestures! He came to buy a few trinkets from our make-shift shop converted from a van. From his accent, he could have been either British or Australian. He had bleached blond hair and a rusty beard. I noticed his eyes the very first time he came to our shop. They were a strange mixture of blue and green. But most important of all they had an expression of sadness around the corners, especially when he smiled. Strange! He showed up a few times and we chatted a bit, not the salesman-customer talk. I was never good at that. He asked me about the nearest town – how far it was. Was there any good hotel to stay at? Then, one afternoon when we closed the awning above our shop and went inside to have lunch and rest, I told my brother,

"I'm going for a walk and will pick up a sandwich somewhere. You don't have to wait for me."

I was distracted by the small Volkswagen bus at the end of the grounds, because of all the stickers on its bumper: Crete, Corsica, Spain, Portugal. Suddenly I felt someone behind me, and I turned around to find the Australian with the sad eyes. He smiled and said, "Hello." He came very close and asked me in a whisper if I knew where he could find a clean toilet. I told him that he could do what I usually did – go to the woods.

"Can you show me where?" He asked.

I told him to follow me since I realized that I needed to go myself. As we stood facing away from each other several feet apart, I thought of my brother; how as children we used to vie with each other about who could pee the longest distance. I was laughing at the memory of it when I saw the Australian coming toward me with his fly open. That was the first time I saw that kind of gesture. I almost ran back to the caravan. When panic subsided, I thought the whole thing over. Actually, I could be friends with him if only he didn't… he had such sad eyes. That was five years ago.

Good, the rest room at the bus station seems to be empty at last. I thought the group of camping kids would never finish. Back in the lobby, I look around again in case my father has come late. By now there are only a handful of people waiting for the last buses, I suppose. Two older women with a young woman and a little boy are in one corner. The boy dozes on a duffel bag, one arm on his mother's lap. Two army men sit on two chairs side by side putting coins into the TV sets attached to their chairs. They seem totally uninvolved with the surroundings or in the TV. No, my father hasn't come. I sit down to think – to decide on my next move. How I hoped he would be here relieving me of this final step. How I dreamed that he would be here to receive me, to welcome me! I have written the date and the time of my arrival clearly in English, in case he has forgotten his German.

No one is behind the sign *Information* at the ticket counter. "May I help you?" the man behind the other window asks.

"Yes, can you please tell me how far Sherman Road is from here?"

"Sherman Road, let's see. Hey, Hank? Do you know how far Sherman Road is?" he asks his neighbor on the other end of the counter.

Hank walks over, looks at me and asks, "Which Sherman Road - in Denver or Aurora?"

I fumble through my wallet to check the address again. I know it by heart. Just in case. I push the piece of paper through the window hole. "Here, here is the full address, please," I say.

Hank and the first man look at the address and then walk to a map on the wall. After a few seconds Hank says pointing a spot on the map, "Here we are. I see it, right there. You can't walk though. It's at least fifteen blocks. Let's see," he pushes his baseball cap off his forehead and looks at the clock on the wall behind me and says, “You may be able to catch the last bus going that way. It’s number 15 behind the station on Main Street.”

“You’ll need exact change,” his colleague adds.

“Thank you very much for your help. I have enough change.” I begin to move toward the door.

“You’re welcome. Where are you from?” Hank asks.

“Europe, Germany. I came to meet….” One of the last buses roars in drowning my last words.

Inside the bus number 15 there are only two other men besides me. They are in some kind of blue uniforms, perhaps waiters or janitors going home after day’s work. Fifteen blocks! Here I am in Denver taking a city bus to Sherman Road where my father lives. It is unbelievable! All these years of plans, saving Marks, searching for his address! Is this really happening! The buses in this country are overheated compared to back home. I stretch my legs out of an aisle seat. Why am I not feeling excited and happy? I am not nervous either! But suddenly I feel an emptiness come over me. Oh, no. Oh, God please, don’t let me have that feeling now! Not now! I wanted to hope, hope for something wonderful; please, don’t let me down.

It was my eighteenth birthday. Mother made my favorite *Schwartzwalder* torte. We had several of our friends from school, my brother Sanjay’s and mine. I had my first schnapps. Uncle Willi insisted that I gulp the whole glass with him.

"You are a man now," he declared, "You don't need to be like your father who did not believe in drinking. He always said, 'Drinking is the worst vice.' You see, in India, men from good families are not supposed to drink alcohol." The strong liquid burned my throat all the way down. I drank some beer to cool off. Soon I felt warm and light-headed.

"Tell me about him, Uncle Willi. What was he like? If he did not drink beer, did he drink only water? Soda?"

Uncle Willi looked at me briefly and looked at my mother who had just put a record on the turntable and approached him. She pulled him by the hand and began to dance in front of the kitchen stove. I looked at her. She was still attractive though slightly chubby. Had my Indian father really loved her? Or was it her exotic look – blond hair and blue eyes – that attracted him? If he really loved her, how could he desert her within three years of their marriage? God! Would I ever get answers to my thousand questions?

Sanjay began to dance disco style to the waltz, and I saw our neighbor's daughter, Melanie, smiling at me from behind the kitchen counter. Again, like many other times before, I pushed aside the thoughts of my father and tried to concentrate on my immediate surroundings.

I smiled back at Melanie, and she came up to me and began moving her hips just under my eyes. I got up from my chair and began to swing with the music. I was warm and happy. And then, suddenly that feeling came all over me without a warning. The cozy kitchen, the waltz on the disc, my mother happy in Uncle Willi's arms, Sanjay dancing with three girls and two boys at the same time and I with beautiful Melanie whose hair was as golden as the best German beer. Everything seemed pointless and nothing seemed to matter.

That evening I thought that the emptiness in my gut had to do with my becoming eighteen. Later I knew that it was not only that. I just have these moods off and on without any warning whatsoever. I learned to live with them as I learned to live without my father.

One thing I have noticed during last five or six years. These moods come unannounced each time I enjoy myself, or begin to, anyway. That time when I went to bed with that Gypsy woman, my first sexual experience, the same thing happened.

It was in that fairground again. The gypsy caravan that summer had a voluptuous woman, who seemed to have an eye for us brothers. We teased each other about her. Then one evening she came running to our shed and talked agitatedly in a foreign tongue. From the few German words she used, we gathered that her dog was missing. I offered to go and help. After about an hour of search everywhere, I was exhausted and shrugged my shoulders gesturing at my watch. She nodded and took my wrist in her hand and led me to her caravan. To our great relief, the dog – a tiny poodle – was standing in front of the cabin! Overjoyed she first cuddled the dog then cuddled and kissed me boldly. She offered me a glass of wine, which was tart and muddy. The evening outside was quiet. People in the fairground retired early. I began to feel tired myself. I was always tired by early evenings anyway. I suppose,

I never liked this business of selling trinkets and cotton prints every summer. But that was the only way I could make some quick money for the journey to find my lost father.

When the gypsy woman poured a second glass of wine for me, I tried to refuse. She held my hand and led me to her bed, a colorful pad of shawls and clothes on top of a long chest. The dog was already on it. She pushed him out gently and pulled me down with her. I lay on my back and remembered seeing a lot of red and magenta and smelling a pungent odor of meat, wine and olive oil.

For many months afterwards, I could not recall anything about our sexual intimacy. Yes, it was my first time, and it was then that I fell into the worst empty mood ever. This time I knew that somehow these empty feelings had something to do with my father. He too does not exist for me, leaving an empty space in my soul; no face, no word, no gesture attached to the words 'my father.' I know now that until I find him I can never enjoy anything in my life. Since then, an urgency to find him has replaced my curiosity.

I had looked everywhere for some sign and information of him. My mother had destroyed everything he had given her. The only thing she ever told me was that he missed his country and his family so much that after Sanjay was born, one day he just left for India, leaving a note saying he'd be back. He never came back, nor did he send an address. It was clear to my mother that he wanted nothing to do with us. She told me once that it took many years for her to get over her loss and anger. I was careful not to ask her too many questions for fear of bringing those feelings back. The only thing he had left us was my brother's name, which he had given him. I think Sanjay was aware that his existence must remind mother of our father. But he never said a word about this to me. Whenever I tried to broach the subject he would leave the room. Perhaps Sanjay does not need my father as much as I do. Or perhaps father's absence is even more painful for him.

Uncle Willi, mother's second cousin, is like a father to both of us and he is the only person who is willing to talk about my father. But he too does not dare to hurt mother by going back to those days. I managed to gather enough bits and pieces of information from him to begin a serious search for my father when I became twenty-one. The urgency to find him kept pressing me. It was not easy. I had to do all this without my mother's or my brother's approval or help.

"If he really wanted to be found, he would have taken some initiative himself, don't you think?" Sanjay would say and I knew he was right. I felt guilty for betraying them, but I had to do it. When at last I located father's address, not in India but in the States, I was overjoyed. I immediately wrote a letter to my father. By then I had saved enough for a round-trip fare on an off-season charter flight to New York. But when his letter came after several months, I wasn't sure anymore. It was lukewarm, neither inviting nor discouraging.

"Dear son,

I'm glad to hear from you and to learn that you all are alive and well. I don't know how I can help you. I left because I had to. Perhaps some day you'll understand and will be able to forgive me."

He signed his full name in the end.

"Next stop, Sherman." The bus-driver's loud voice cuts through my musings. I get off the bus and look at my wristwatch in the light of the streetlamp. It's already eleven. Is it a good idea to knock on a stranger's door at this hour even if he is my father? What if he hasn't received my letter? What if he has and does not wish to see me?

A brief walk brings me to the end of the street in front of a small house. A thin film of snow has gathered on the roof, the railing and the mailbox. I barely make out the number on the mailbox; it's not his number. It must be the next house. Then I see a door to the left of this house. The glass window next to it shows a dim light. No second house and no number on this side door. The damp stink of rotten garbage tells me that there must be a dumping ground very close. Where is the number? I knock on the door next to the dimly lit window. A few seconds later an elderly man opens the door a little.

"Excuse me sir, I am very sorry to bother you at this hour. I'm looking for 215 A Sherman Road. The number here is 215." I say nervously.

"This is 215 A," the old voice says, and the door opens several inches more.

I hear myself saying, "I am Peter from Germany. Haven't you received my letter?" The old man opens the door all the way and lets me in.

"Oh, yes. Come in. It's late. I… I thought…" He does not finish what he wants to say and begins to close the door behind us. I hesitate. My father does not greet me with a handshake or in any other way. I follow him to the first room, which looks like a kitchen. He walks over to the gas stove and puts a pot of water on. He limps a little. He is not as tall as I had imagined. His hair is thin and still dark. I can't see his face. I put my pack down and pull one of the wooden chairs from under the table and sit. My father takes two mugs from an open shelf and puts some instant coffee in them and pours hot water. He says, "I don't have any cream or milk. Do you mind?"

"No." I pick up the coffee cup. We sit face to face. I do not know what to say. I have a hard time believing he is my father. It must be a mistake. I feel very tired.

After we drink the coffee in silence he gathers the two mugs to the sink and says, "Do you want anything else? It's getting late. I need to go to bed. You can use the little room. The bathroom is over there." He points to his left and before walking out of the kitchen adds, "we can talk tomorrow."

Next morning when I awake I realize I am in a strange place. My body aches all over. But I have slept on the floor before. It must be the long journey. The charter flight was crammed and the long bus ride from New York was uncomfortable. I turn inside my sleeping bag and then crawl out of it. A blast of cold draft slaps my naked body. I dress quickly in the other set of clothes I have brought with me. A pair of flannel trousers Sanjay gave me last Christmas and the red sweater Mother has knitted for my twenty-fourth birthday this year. I have worn it only once. When I enter the kitchen, I see my father hovering over the stove like last night.

"Would you like some coffee? Some bread? I don't have anything else, need to go shopping," he says slowly.

"Good morning." I say and look at him. In the daylight I can see him better. His eyes are on the loaf of bread he is holding.

"You don't have ten bucks on you, by any chance? I need to buy some tablets for my arthritis. I… I don't have money to buy food to offer you. You have come from such a distance…." He trails off. I fumble through my wallet and take out my last fifty dollars, put the bills on the table without looking at him. "Why have you come, Sanjay? I can't give you anything, not even breakfast. My social security check hasn't arrived this month. My wife left me ten years ago and took my daughters away." He tries to break a piece of bread without looking at me.

"I want to say, Papa, you had left us many years before. And I am not Sanjay, I am Peter your youngest son who was two when you left. You were in such a rush to leave for your country, but you are in America. What happened?"

But I cannot bring myself to say any of this or ask him a thousand other questions, which have been festering inside me all my life and finally have brought me to his door. Instead, I swallow the black coffee without milk and sugar. It is cold in the kitchen.

We sit at the table for a long time. The familiar emptiness comes creeping back. Everything seems out of place, especially me in this cold kitchen in front of this stranger who is my father.

Slowly I get up from the chair and tell him, "My name is Peter, Peter Schmidt. Do you remember my mother's last name?" I put the empty coffee cup over the dollar bills and walk out with my backpack. I do not say goodbye to my father.

As I wait for the bus, my eyes begin to burn. The cold wind blows hard on my face and nearly dries the tears, which begin to roll down to the collar of the red sweater Mother made for my birthday. I do not feel like taking my hands out of the warm pockets to wipe the tears. I blink to read the number of the bus that is approaching. Yes, I need to catch number 15 again and go back to the bus station. Perhaps Hank and his colleague will help me find some odd job to make enough to buy a ticket to New York. Thank God, I have the return air-ticket from there.

Ever since I returned from my trip to America, I felt free of my obsession with my father and somehow the emptiness in my soul seemed to have disappeared. I thank my father for this unexpected gift.

My Mother

When I heard that my mother was diagnosed with breast cancer I was really shocked because we never saw her sick with anything, not even mild fever or a cold in the winter. I realized that I had to find a way to have a heart-to-heart talk with her. The need for such a talk drove me most of my life, but something always kept me from it. How would I live with myself if I lost my last chance? My husband, who is a doctor, reassured me that a diagnosis of breast cancer today is not necessarily a death sentence.

What I really needed to ask her was why she was always so critical of me. I also needed to tell her how many nights I wept myself to sleep from the pain of her constant disapproval – an ache that still exists somewhere inside my heart. I never understood why she could not love me. Is it because I was my father's favorite? At some point my tears turned into anger and I became someone my mother could dislike with good reasons. The more she criticized me the more I defied her. At the same time, I tried everything I could for her slightest approval. I began to study very hard at school and did extremely well. I heard from the neighbors and relatives later that she was proud of my academic achievements but she never acknowledged it to me.

By the time I went to college, I turned into an expert debater and argued with my mother like an experienced prosecutor. My need for her approval seemed to have reduced considerably and now it was all out war about everything. One day during summer vacation, when I was home from college, my mother handed me an open envelope addressed to me.

"Who is this letter from? What awful language! Is that what they teach you in college nowadays?" Her tone was hot with anger.

"How dare you open my letter? I'm nineteen years old and you can't control my life anymore." I said as I snatched the envelope from her hand.

"Oh, you've become too independent, ha? Wait till I tell your father."

"Go right ahead. He'll understand my need for privacy. You know what? Next year I shall go to my friend Reba's home for my vacation. Her parents love and accept me for who I am." I left the room fuming, giving her no opportunity to continue.

That evening I noticed an extra piece of my favorite fish on my dinner plate. Mother's peace-offering!

By now I realized that perhaps most of her reactions to me had little to do with her love for me. For some inexplicable reasons, my mother was incapable of showing her love, which she nurtured deep inside. For her the hardest thing was to let her children grow up and go beyond the orbit of her own rules of gravity. My brother followed the system, I rebelled. And unlike my father I could not forgive her just because she had an over-protective love for her family.

These clashes continued until I left home after marrying someone of whom she initially disapproved. The day I was to leave, Mother was nowhere to be seen. I went upstairs and knocked on my parents' bedroom door.

"Ma, we're ready to leave. Aren't you coming out?"

"Yes, in a minute." Her voice sounded heavy with tears. I waited. A few minutes later she opened the door. I forced a smile and hesitated. We stood with barely a yard of space between us, but neither my mother nor I crossed it to give a hug. After a few seconds she said, "Have a safe trip and don't forget to call when you get there." I heard my husband calling from downstairs and I left in a hurry.

On the way to the airport I kept thinking that my mother arranged for us to be alone before my departure, yet neither of us could cross over the chasm of misunderstandings that had widened for twenty odd years.

And, now this awful news of her cancer! I must make an effort to communicate. I needed her to know that I sort of understood where she was coming from. I sat down and wrote a scenario of our meeting; stood in front of the mirror and rehearsed the whole conversation. I called home saying that I would like to come for a visit soon. Mother sounded weak but calm. She asked if my husband would accompany me. I said I would come alone.

By the time I managed to get there, she was hospitalized. The cancer had metastasized. She looked a little pale but otherwise unchanged. I sat on the only chair next to her bed. Father left the room with the excuse of getting a cup of coffee. I touched her palm, which was limp and cool. I realized then that I had never touched my mother since I was seven. I held her hand as we chatted about trivia. All my rehearsed conversation evaporated. I could not tell her any of that. Perhaps she knew what I wanted to say. It suddenly occurred to me that perhaps all her admonitions and criticisms were the only way she was able to show her feelings. Even if I was wrong, it felt good to come to this conclusion. I began to feel sorry for my mother more than I felt sad that she might die.

That night in bed I prayed for a long time for my mother's recovery. She died a month later in her sleep. I never could sit down with my mother and have a talk after all. But I like to think that she understood my need to do so anyway. The other thought that still occurs to me and breaks my heart is that perhaps she suffered more than I did.

The Betel Quid

Eleven-year-old Nina likes to be in the day bed with the women of the family, who lounge every summer afternoon after the midday meal of rice and curry. The two aunts, Maya and Jaya, are her mother's married sisters, who, like her mother, are visiting their parents' home for the summer. Nina squeezes herself in between the edge of the bed and her younger aunt's opulent thighs in the wide king-size bed covered with woven palm-leaf mat to keep it cool. Usually, she joins the grown-ups a few minutes after they settle in with pillows under their bulging breasts and between legs. They hardly notice her entrance to their adult world. The ladies talk with their mouths full of betel quid. Nina needs to concentrate hard to follow their words soaked in the juice of the story and the betel leaf. Their eyelids appear heavier as the afternoon descends on them and they chew the potent betel. But the sleep is yet to come.

"And then she screamed saying horrible things about his family." Grandma says as she puts her index finger inside her mouth picking something from her left molar, perhaps a piece of the betel leaf. Nina nudges closer not to miss anything. She has still to catch the thread of the story.

"What exactly did she say?" Nina's mother asks in a drowsy voice.

"I can't repeat. These are words for the witch's ears. Things like…" Grandma casts a look around and Nina immediately flattens herself under her aunt Jaya's sari and covers her head under a pillow. Grandma lowers her voice and whispers, "She said that he didn't have a big enough – you know what – to give her pleasure…" She stops, extends her half-stretched body out of the edge of the bed and picks up the brass pot from the floor and spits mouthful of red betel juice in it before putting it down again. Aunt Maya raises her head from her pillow, turns toward grandma and supports her head on her right palm before saying,

"My, my! What guts!! Married barely two years and she's already complaining. If only she knew what it's like to be married for fifteen years and be pregnant for five times. Pleasures! Who says men ever cared about their wives' pleasures? Hah!"

"What happened then?" Aunt Jaya sounds impatient.

Grandma turns her hot pillow over and continues, "He stomped out of the room muttering things and she called out after him, 'I'm going to my parents' for a month. I can only take this torture in small doses.' 'Suit yourself,' he said and left the house. The maid saw the wife pressing her sari on her eyes sobbing."

Nina's mother and aunts change their positions and lay down closing their eyes, perhaps wondering how to get the next installment of the story from the neighbor's maid.

Nina lies awake wondering about whom they are talking, the next-door neighbors who have moved to the neighborhood recently? Are they talking about sex? She wishes she could be part of the group and ask grandma some questions. For now, she has to be satisfied with only bits and pieces. She lies next to one of her aunts and smells the pungent smell of her sweat and talcum powder. Her grandmother is already snoring a little. Something vague, like the story she just heard, keeps her glued to the bed of these women of two generations and older, who share a forbidden and enchanting world where Nina is not yet allowed to enter. Nina lies still and dreams of the days when she too will take part in the juicy gossip and the betel quid. Until then she has to sneak into it, catching only words of innuendoes and making up her own stories as she pleases.

Stalemate

"Although your wife has uterine cancer, it's only stage one and hasn't spread. The whole uterus was removed. We do not see any need for further treatment. Still, I shall discuss with my colleagues in radiotherapy and oncology in case they recommend additional treatment. Right now, she needs to recover from the hysterectomy." I was watching the doctor closely and detected no anxiety on her expression.

I came a week ago from Mumbai to help Ruma out during her surgery. My husband and I live and work in Mumbai. Our only son is away in England studying medicine. Ruma and Bikash's only daughter Soma is at Carnegie Mellon studying engineering.

Ruma was released from the hospital after two weeks. Bikash told the maid Malati to sweep and mop the small guest room next to the living room on the first floor. This room has an attached half bath, and the kitchen is only a few steps in one direction and the living room in another. I helped Malati to make Ruma's bed with fresh sheets, pillowcases, and a light quilt. Bikash remembered to put a bunch of fragrant tuberoses – Ruma's favorite flower – in the tall vase standing at the corner of the room. He even put a few family photos on the small dressing table with drawers, that was brought down from their bedroom. Their daughter Soma smiled from her photo. The whole staff including the driver, cook, maid and the gardener all stood at the front door to welcome their mistress as if she was returning from a long trip. After two weeks at the hospital Ruma looked pale but rested.

"Nice! I can see and hear everything from my bed," Ruma said with a faint smile, "I can even watch TV in the living room whenever I feel like it." Soon my sister developed a daily routine. She hardly complained of any discomfort. Surprisingly, within a week she began to gain her strength back. When visitors gathered in the living room, she joined in conversations occasionally from her bed. Her close friends came inside and sat around her bed. A nurse came for the first couple of weeks to bathe and dress her and to give her medicines. She combed Ruma's hair in a loose bun, watched TV with her until noon and fed her lunch. Then the nurse had a cup of tea and left with her handbag and a lady's parasol. Within ten days Ruma let the nurse go with the excuse that she was well enough to take care of her basic physical needs. "You don't want me to be an invalid, do you?" she told her husband with an endearing smile. I breathed a sigh of relief seeing my sister back to her wonderful, independent self.

Every afternoon I spent a few hours with Ruma, sometimes watching her favorite soap on TV and talking about it afterwards. I helped her comb her long hair and gossiped with her about distant family members. I tried to make her laugh trying to say something even remotely funny.

Bikash returned from court around seven in the evening, always something in his hand – a bouquet of flowers or a chocolate cake from the bakery in New Market or a new book of short stories by Ruma's favorite author. He went upstairs to change into something comfortable before coming down to be with his wife. Ruma waited for him to have the evening tea and home-made snacks together. The rest of the family disappeared, giving them a chance to be alone before visitors started pouring in. All of us were aware that Bikash and Ruma did not share their bed right now; they needed more private time together. The love between my sister and her husband was well-known in our family. When they were young, we joked and teased them about it; now after Ruma's surgery it's a different story.

"You're looking really fresh today, Ruma," Bikash said one evening when they had tea together. "How are you feeling? Do you want more books? Does reading tire you? Oh, I almost forgot to tell you that one of our handymen from the court will come tomorrow to set up a small TV set on the wall so that you can watch your favorite soaps right from your bed."

"What for? The nurse assured me before she left that I can move upstairs by next week. Besides, I can walk a few steps to the living room to watch the TV if I want. I could use a CD player, though. I'd love to listen to some of Tagore's songs," Ruma said as her husband held her hand.

"That's easy. Your sister can get you a CD player." He then called me and said, "Tomorrow after I reach the court I shall send the car back. I shall explain to the driver where some good electronic stores are. Please take some cash from the second drawer of the bureau in the upstairs bedroom and get a good set. Buy also some CDs with it. You know what your sister likes."

When I retire to my little room on the third-floor attic every night and lay on my lonely bed, I wonder about Ruma's good luck of having such an attentive and loving husband. Even after twenty-three years of marriage Bikash's attention and concerns remain like it was in the first year of their lives together. And I! I have come over a month from Mumbai and I got only two phone calls from my husband! I wonder if he would remember my birthday next week. A faint twinge of jealousy hit me. I know I should not feel this way. After all, my sister is recovering from a major surgery.

One morning, four weeks after Ruma moved upstairs to their bedroom, she did not come down to breakfast. I waited for her and wanted to discuss my plan to return to Mumbai. My leave of absence from my college would be over soon and I needed to return to my job and my household. When she did not come down even at ten o'clock I climbed up to their room and knocked gently.

"Come in," she said. She was still in bed and tried to raise herself but had a grimace. I asked if she was alright. She smiled faintly and said, "I don't know what's wrong. I seem to have a sudden weakness and a numb pain. It's nothing to worry about." She got up a bit later and came down after a shower. She skipped breakfast saying, "It's late, I shall have lunch early," and ordered her favorite dishes to be prepared. But at lunch I noticed she was not that hungry. I did not make any comments. We talked about this and that. For some reason I did not broach the subject of my return. Ruma's appetite did not return and by the third week after this event, I could not help noticing how thin she looked.

Two and a half months had passed since her hysterectomy but Ruma showed little interest in going back to her job or anything else for that matter. I had a feeling she was not telling us everything. One evening Bikash complained about her not eating her dinner. She excused herself saying that she had a late lunch and was not hungry. I made up my mind to talk to Bikash about it behind her back. I was becoming concerned. Then one morning she was late for breakfast again. I asked Malati to take up a breakfast tray to the upstairs bedroom and followed her.

I was shocked to find Ruma lying in a fetal position clasping her tummy complaining of terrible pain. I called Dr. Basu's number and left a message with her nurse. Dr. Basu called back within ten minutes and suggested we take her to the surgeon Dr. Agarwala's office at 11 AM. She had already made an appointment for us. I knew Bikash had an important case in court that morning. I called his secretary to say that Malati and I were taking Ruma to the hospital. He should come to the surgeon's office as soon as possible. Dr.

Agarwala examined Ruma carefully and prescribed several tests including a full body scan and an abdominal ultrasound. I noticed a slight frown between his eyebrows. I did not recall if he had it always or if it had just appeared after examining Ruma.

The clock kept ticking. Around one o'clock Bikash called to find out the update. He said he'd come to the hospital as soon as he could. Around 2 PM I gave Malati a few rupees to take a taxi home. Ruma was not allowed to eat anything except some medicated liquid. When she was in one of her tests, I walked around and found a cafeteria and had a cup of strong coffee and a piece of toast. I'd lost my appetite. By the time all the tests were done it was close to six in the evening. Bikash called my mobile phone a few more times to make sure we were still at the hospital and came to pick us up at six thirty. Poor Ruma was exhausted and held on to him in the back seat of the car when we finally headed home. Dr. Agarwala promised to call us the next day with the test results.

"Do you still have pain, Ruma?" I asked

"No, but I'm extremely tired," she said. Her voice was hardly audible.

"If you're hungry, how about stopping at your favorite restaurant on the way home? Would you like that?" Bikash asked in his most tender voice and looked at his wife's bent head on his shoulder.

"I'm not hungry, really. Let's go home. I may have a long glass of *lassi*. Malati makes it the way I like," I heard her say from the back seat. I felt sorry for Bikash. He must be starved after the whole day's work and sick with worry as well. That night we had some snacks, home-made yogurt and pieces of pears and apples. I went to my bedroom on the third floor and fell into a disturbed sleep. Is the cancer back? Was the last thought I had before falling asleep.

The next morning by the time I awoke, showered, dressed and came downstairs, Bikash was already on the phone in the front veranda talking in a low voice, I guess, out of Ruma's earshot. Looking at his face I knew the news was not good. I heard him say,

"When can you start the chemo? Is it really necessary to wait? Yes, yes, I understand she needs to get stronger before the treatment. I do. But please try to understand my side of it..." He trailed off. Closing the phone, he looked at me and told me the worst we all anticipated. Ruma's cancer not only came back, it spread to her colon and liver. At breakfast, I wanted to ask the inevitable question of how it could have have happened. Her gynecologist assured us that the hysterectomy was the right treatment to get rid of the cancer which was localized. Like many rational queries, this too sounded irrelevant at this point of time and seemed like a pretence to stay away from the truth of the dire prognosis. The doctors were only capable within their limits. Cancer is far bigger and menacing than any expert prognosis. Looking at Bikash's face my heart broke. I wish I knew how to console him. Somehow right now his agony seemed far worse than my concerns for my sister. I felt relieved that I was not in his shoes, and I did not have to tell Ruma the devastating news. After a brief chat with Ruma and the maids I went to the garden and sat there in the morning sun pretending to read the daily newspaper.

Small events from our childhood kept floating in like vague hypnogogic visions. My jealous feelings when I first saw her in the hospital after she was born – our fights over the toys and one particular celluloid doll with golden hair that our uncle brought from London for me. He did not know about Ruma's birth. Mother urged me to share it with my little sister, but it seemed so unfair on top of the fact that ever since she arrived in this world she usurped nearly all my rights. I was amazed at the power of such a little thing! However, by the time she entered first grade at the same school as mine I became her protective older sister. I'd learned the satisfaction of being the magnanimous older sibling and that never stopped.

I wished as her older sister I could make the cancer go away. I was grateful our parents were not alive to witness their beloved youngest child's predicament. The morning sun had touched my feet and began to climb up my body and I began to feel hot. I knew I had to face my sister, otherwise she would guess something was terribly wrong.

Bikash appeared on the veranda all dressed to leave for the court and said, "Uma, I told Ruma that she'll need prophylactic treatment, and this will begin soon. I do not believe she suspects anything. Please don't say anything about the metastasis, not yet. I want her to be hopeful and enjoy her life as long as possible." At the end of the sentence his voice cracked a little. I came closer, touched his arm and whispered to him,

"Please, Bikash, try to get hold of yourself. If you lose courage and hope, she'll feel it and lose hers too. We can't let that happen," I said trying to push my tears back down my throat. Bikash simply nodded before getting into the car that was waiting on the driveway.

That evening at Bikash's invitation I joined him and Ruma for a light dinner and we talked about this and that to keep the tone light. Ruma did not complain of any physical discomfort; she even asked me if she and I could go to a morning show of a rerun of her favorite Hollywood western, *Dodge City*, which was being shown at one of the downtown cinemas. She saw the ad in that morning's newspaper. This made both her husband and me laugh. I got up with my empty plate with the excuse of fetching some water to hide my teary eyes. Ruma was succeeding in distracting us instead of us doing it for her.

That night from my lonely bed I called my husband on my mobile and told him the situation. He was shocked and sympathetic but also urged me to go back at least for awhile if possible. Instead of telling me how much he missed me he gave a list of household things waiting for my attention. At another time I'd have caught him in his trick and mentioned it but now I did not have the mood for any such levity. The sudden turn of Ruma's condition spread a pall – a dark spell over us. Our existence was tied to her fate and future. At my husband's insistence, I agreed to go back for a visit, provided that Bikash agreed, I told him. After I shut off my phone I wept bitterly for my sister's impending death. Or perhaps the tears were for us, the so-called survivors.

The next morning, a Thursday, right after Bikash left the house for work, my mobile phone rang. It was Dr. Anima Bose, Ruma's primary physician. She said,

"I cannot seem to reach your brother-in-law. Please convey to him what I have to say. My colleagues – Ruma's surgeon, the radiotherapist and the oncologist all came to the conclusion that the treatment should not wait any longer. They propose four weeks of radiotherapy – five days a week followed by chemotherapy after a break of one week if she tolerates the radiotherapy well. Usually, most patients feel no immediate side effects. The chemotherapy will follow – possibly three sets covering several weeks, with breaks after each week. It's an ambitious plan and they may have to adjust the regimen depending on her tolerance. She needs to start the radiotherapy this coming Monday. Please make sure she is at the cancer center by 8 AM. Any questions?" Dr. Bose stopped as if to take a breath. I tried to store the information in my brain and had not enough time to process any of the implications. I thanked her and said,

"I shall call Bikash right away and tell him what you said. By the way, I do have a question. Do you think we should tell Ruma about her metastasis? Don't we need to explain the reason why she needs this elaborate treatment?" A voice inside me blurted out.

"You mean you haven't told Ruma yet? Okay, I shall call her over the weekend and explain the situation. What's a good time to call?" Dr. Bose asked.

"I don't know if Bikash will like the idea of telling Ruma. I'm sorry I mentioned it," I said, beginning to feel guilty for betraying Bikash. Perhaps guessing my dilemma, Dr. Bose quickly said,

"I have to go now. Let me think about it. I shall talk to Bikash later about this. But make sure Ruma is at the clinic on Monday morning." She said quickly and cut the line. I too shut the phone and kept looking at it as if it might talk back to help me. I walked out in the garden and pressed Bikash's number. He picked up the phone immediately. I gave him Dr. Bose's message and also added that I'd like to make a brief trip to Mumbai over the weekend and would return Sunday night. I needed to take care of a few things there.

"Once Ruma's treatment starts I want to stay put." I added.

"Of course! I have been so preoccupied with your sister that I haven't even thought of your needs. That's a good idea. When do you want to go? My secretary can book you a seat at any flight tomorrow."

"Not tomorrow. I prefer to leave this afternoon. The sooner I go, the sooner I can return. I shall tell Ruma a white lie about my sudden departure – I shall think of something.

Please tell your secretary to get a return flight no later than Sunday evening. Thanks, Bikash."

Before I left for Mumbai, Bikash urged me to bring my husband back with me. Perhaps he was worried that our physical separation would cut my stay with them short. When Sandip met me at the Mumbai airport, he was very pleased by my sudden arrival. I did not tell him ahead of time that I was coming for the weekend. We had three days of bittersweet reunion. He could see that I was totally preoccupied with my worry about Ruma. He knew the gravity of the matter and was sympathetic. But when I asked if he'd go back with me for a short visit, he was very upset. He thought I came back for good. I knew it would be impossible for him to leave his job even briefly at a short notice. He became a bit distant when he heard that I planned to return after three days. How I hoped that my husband would hold me tight when I wept about my sister's impending death. He consoled me by saying,

"Modern medicine can do miracles. Don't you think you're being a bit melodramatic!"

When I left he was at work. I took a cab to the airport and wept quietly through the flight. I could not help remembering all the small exchanges between my brother-in-law and my dying sister. I could not help comparing our two marriages!

Ruma's radiation treatment went off without a hitch. However, her abdominal pain came back and the discomfort due to pain kept up. But Ruma never complained. When we were growing up she was everyone's favorite because of her sweet nature. I adored my little sister but was secretly jealous. I always felt I was being punished because of my feisty and perky nature. At school my teachers loved me because of my intelligence and 'always ready for anything' attitude. Ruma was relatively shy and quiet but popular among the relatives. She was never any trouble and now we all are postponing our lives to be by her side. My love for my sister increased a hundred fold because of her illness. None of us think she'll be cured of this horrific disease, but none of us dare think it aloud, even inside our own heads, lest we allow it to happen.

When Bikash and I are alone we never mention Ruma's cancer. We talk a lot about the logistics, the doctors and medical appointments or anything we can do to see even a flicker of Ruma's smile. Our lives' goal right now is to help her forget her condition even for a few seconds. Poor, poor Ruma! It does not make any sense why a lovely and lovable person like her is being punished like this. Whatever little jealousy I felt about her seems to have vanished now. I wish I knew how to prepare myself for her death which seems more and more a definite possibility. The question is 'when'?

Ruma had two courses of her chemo and tolerated them better than we expected. She no longer complained about pain but had lost a lot of weight, her skin lost the luster but her eyes still carried a keen force of life. She never said it, but I knew that she wanted to live a long life. I also knew that like all of us, she realized her days were numbered. Bikash and I were with her all through the treatments. We even tried to celebrate the endings of each course of chemotherapy with a little party among ourselves and a few relatives who still frequented two or three times a week. But their visits had changed in structure. After a few words of "How are you feeling?" "Do you need anything?" "Do you want to eat anything in particular?" they left with one excuse or another. Only Bikash continued to come back from work with a bouquet of Ruma's favorite flowers or a box of her favorite chocolates and tried to make small talk to make her forget her fateful future. I knew what kind of inhuman efforts he had to master to pretend that what Ruma had to suffer was temporary. He had no choice. He had to do this, not only to make Ruma forget the awful prognosis, but also to save himself from the same knowledge even for a brief time.

We – Ruma, her husband, the relatives who still visited regularly and I – all of us seemed to have joined in a conspiracy not to mention the disease, as if not uttering that six-letter word would magically avert the inevitable. We were somewhat paralyzed between an extremely unlikely hope against hope of the patient's survival and the more likely prognosis of impending death. No one had the courage to say, "Ruma will get better." Even her doctors seemed afraid to say anything about the disease lest the spell of hope shattered. This precarious balance between hope of life and despair of death could not continue for long. One evening to my surprise Bikash said to me,

"I don't know how long I can pay for the medical bills. All my savings including the retirement fund is about to be depleted." He caught himself and changed the topic by saying, "All that matters is Ruma's wellbeing. I shall borrow money if I have to. By the way, Uma, does she talk to you about death?"

"No, never." I was still thinking about Bikash's earlier comment. I had never heard him worry or even mention money. He was known as the most generous human being who opened his wallet before anyone else. Was he really worried about the expenses? Or was he getting tired of the situation. I wondered.

Ruma seemed totally oblivious of all our feelings and reactions. One afternoon when I was combing her long tresses, suddenly a clump of hair came off her head. I was so shocked that I forgot to continue combing. Ruma had the most beautiful hair in the family. Everyone praised her long wavy hair which felt like silk to touch. She always wore her hair in a loose bun and decorated it with a spring of fresh jasmine every evening before Bikash came home from work. Ruma turned her head toward me and said in a normal voice,

"Dr. Bose told me last time that I may lose all my hair – the usual result of the chemotherapy. She also said the hair will grow back after the treatment is over. It's a small price to pay for a cure, don't you think?" She smiled at me in a way as if she was consoling me. I shoved the clumps of my sister's lost hair in a cloth bag and tried hard to push back my tears that made a burning sensation behind my eyes. I could not help thinking, 'what's the source of her strength? How can this increasingly emaciated body hold such fortitude and courage?'

A couple of days later Ruma asked me, "Could you please bring Bikash's shaving razor from the upstairs bathroom and shave my head? If I keep losing hair in clumps why not make it easier by getting rid of it all? I think I may even look fashionable like those French performers, ladies who crop their hair very short. What do you think?" I complied but not before asking Bikash's permission. He just shrugged and sounded resigned when he said,

"If that's what she wants, why not? I love her long hair but at this point I just want her to have whatever she wants." After the shave, Ruma looked like a sickly boy, not at all fashionable. I did my best to keep the hand mirror away from her.

Just before the end of her chemotherapy Ruma developed a severe pain on her back. The CT scan revealed metastasis on her spine and there were a few fractures on the vertebra. Her oncologist discussed the futility of any aggressive treatment at this stage and gave a packet of morphine patch to Bikash if needed. He said, "I'm so, so sorry" and left the room. I noticed that the doctor averted any eye contacts with us.

On the way home Bikash and I sat on the back seat of the car without a word. Finally, at a stop light, Bikash looked out the window at the flow of people rushing in all directions and said,

"Uma, you have been such a help to your sister and all of us, especially to me. I do not know how I could handle anything without you on my side. But maybe you need to think of getting back to your life. Sandip has been extremely patient. I'm eternally grateful to him. You heard what the oncologist said. We must face the reality." He could not continue, stopped and cleared his throat.

"Please Bikash, let's see a few more days how Ruma is. She is your wife, the love of your life. But don't forget she's also my baby sister, my only living sibling." I could not hold back my tears. Bikash held my left hand with his right tightly and blew his nose into his handkerchief with the other hand. We began to mourn Ruma even before she breathed her last. The car turned into the driveway of the house. Bikash turned toward me and said matter-of-factly,

"I shall call Soma tomorrow to come to see her mother. I haven't told her about the seriousness of Ruma's condition. I did not want her to worry, but things are different now."

"I was thinking the same," I said.

Soma, Ruma and Bikash's only daughter, who studied in Pittsburgh, USA, came within two days and stayed a week. She was so shocked to see her mother's condition that she scolded her father and me for not letting her know. She was angry with the doctors, with her father and all of us, finally leaving with the excuse that she had an important exam to take. Ruma looked at her daughter but said nothing when Soma entered her room to say 'goodbye' before she left. I tried to explain why Soma left, but Ruma raised her palm to stop me and asked for some tea. She must have guessed that her daughter came all the way from America to see her for the last time. She never asked me or Bikash about our meeting with the oncologist. I was sure she knew the prognosis.

Ruma seemed to have made a decision. She started to behave as normal as one could under the circumstances. Whenever the pain attacked her, she asked me or Bikash to administer the morphine patch. Surprisingly she still walked to the living room every afternoon with the help of her cane and watched her favorite soap! She even looked close to normal. Her hair had grown back, although she wore it cropped. A strange determination to live showed through her every behavior. She never mentioned her disease when relatives dropped in occasionally. She talked only about herself – her new hair and the fact that she looked so young. I could not help noticing how my kind generous sister had turned into a totally self-absorbed person or was it her total denial of death! I could no longer figure her out. She had even begun to neglect her loving husband and had stopped caring if he came home in the evening or not. He, on the other hand, kept up his nursing as before bringing her favorite flowers and a new gift every evening when he came home after work.

Sandip, my husband, in the meantime managed to get a transfer to their Kolkata office and was now staying with us at Bikash and Ruma's home. I didn't need to sleep in my bed alone anymore. Now I had someone to talk to freely and I could weep quietly on his lap. But none of us talked freely about one thing. We did not dare say a word about how exhausted we all were waiting for Ruma to die. It was thirteen months since her first diagnosis and four months since the metastasis. The doctors did not predict how long she might live. None of us uttered the forbidden word, yet it was all around us. We wanted to have a timeline. How long did we have to wait! All of our lives were on hold. Yet all of us would give anything to assure that Ruma lived a long healthy life. But we knew better. This uncertainty between the sure death and our desire to see her cured and well was killing us.

Death seemed to be enjoying a cruel game – Ruma on one side and death on the other. Ruma seemed to be in a stale mate with death, but it appeared as if they had some sort of understanding. None of us onlookers knew the rules of the game but wanted the game to be over. We were near death ourselves from exhaustion of hopelessness and guilt of the secret wish that death ought to win sooner than later.

Madeleine

My close friend Jacqueline called me one Wednesday morning and asked if I'd be so kind as to move to her home for one or two nights. She needed someone to stay with her 5-year-old daughter Madeleine while she was with her 2-year-old son Riki at the hospital. Riki was already there with sudden high fever on top of his chronic asthma and his pediatrician wanted to keep him in the hospital for observation for a few days before trying any new treatment. The doctor was cautious because several children in our town had shown signs of childhood meningitis!

"Jonathan had to go to Washington on business yesterday before all this happened and he won't be back until the weekend. I don't want to interrupt his business trip unless it's a real emergency," Jacqueline added. Her voice betrayed real anxiety even though she tried hard to hide it.

'How can I refuse a good friend a request like this,' I told myself, although I do not like her daughter that much. Madeleine is quite precocious and her adult manner of speech often puts me off. Well, it may be just one night or at the most two. She'll sleep in her room and I in the guest room. "Of course I can stay with Madie. Don't you worry. When do you want me there?" I asked. Fortunately, I did not have any important appointments for the next day or two. "Anytime after 4, say 5ish? Thank you, thank you so much, Nita. I owe you one. By the way, I explained everything to Madie; she is very excited to spend the night with you. She asked if you'll tell her stories about the god with the elephant head. Could you please?" Before I could respond Jacqueline hung up.

When I arrived a few minutes before 5, I saw Jacqueline backing her car out of the garage in a hurry. She handed me a piece of paper with the security code of the front door of the house and quickly explained a few household details. Before rolling up the car window she said "I shall call you tonight when I get a chance. Thanks again. Bye."

"Good luck!" I said after the car was halfway out of the driveway.

I entered their one-storey, ranch-style house and looked for Madeleine and found her lying on her stomach on her bed supporting herself on a pillow with her two elbows watching cartoons on the TV. Without moving she smiled at me and said,

"Mom wants us to eat macaroni and cheese for dinner. If you need my help to make it just holler." She grabbed a teddy bear and went back to her TV again as if my presence there was a normal event.

In the kitchen, first I had to unload the dishwasher before reloading the remaining dirty dishes in the sink. I managed to find the ingredients of our dinner and made macaroni and cheese. I was about to call Madeleine when she showed up.

"I better tell you that I have a plan for our activities after dinner. I like to hear stories when I eat my ice cream. You will tell me stories of your elephant-headed god, right? When I feel sleepy from the stories then we share the bed in the guest room. It's a queen-size bed, so no problem, because I tend to move a lot when I sleep." She drew a chair near the table and sat on it, ready to eat. I could not help noticing that she said all this without any opportunity for any interruptions or questions.

"I too have a plan of our activities after dinner which is slightly different from yours." I said trying to look at her eyes. I continued, "First, you'll help me clean up by showing me where all the dry dishes go. Then you'll take a bath. After the bath you may have your warm milk with or without chocolate. There is no ice cream in the freezer. I shall be happy to read any story you want me to read from your pile of books. And, you will sleep in your own bed. I'm sorry, I cannot sleep with anyone else." I ended narrating my plan and tried to make eye contact again. This time she looked up but kept quiet a few seconds before saying to nobody in particular,

"I wish I was in the hospital! Why can't you tell me a story? Just one, p-l-e-a-s-e. I told my friends that I'll tell them about your god." She looked directly at me with such imploring eyes that it melted my heart. I scolded myself silently for being so hard on a little girl. It's just her manner of speech beyond her age that made me forget her age!

"Okay. I'll tell you one story after you finish your bath and have your milk. Remember you'll have to go to sleep after that."

"Deal," She stretched her right hand to strike high five. I drew her bath when she finished her meal.

When Madeleine appeared in the guest room after her bath and in her pajamas, she looked like an angel. She had her mother's blonde wavy hair which was now wet and her father's dark blue eyes and pale complexion.

"This is the coziest room in the house, don't you think? We'll go under the blanket. That way you won't be cold when you tell the story. If I feel sleepy you can take me in your arms and put me in my bed if you insist. My Dad does that whenever I fall asleep in the living room," Madeleine said. I began to feel quite sorry for her. She must be lonely without her parents and her little brother. It cannot be easy to spend the night with a non-relative, a stranger. I began to feel guilty for being so hard on her earlier. I got a towel from my bathroom and dried her wet hair and combed it carefully leaving the tangles alone. We went to bed under the blanket.

As I was about to begin the story of how Ganesh, the son of the goddess Durga got an elephant's head, the phone rang. Madeleine jumped up from bed in an instant and ran to the living room to fetch the cordless phone. She was talking to her mother as she came back to the guest room. Perhaps from her mother's insistence, she reluctantly handed over the receiver to me.

Jacqueline told me that Riki's fever is down, the blood test result is promising; nothing serious was found. They will return home tomorrow after breakfast. Could I stay until they come back?

"Of course," I said. Thanking me one more time Jacqueline left the phone. Happily, I relayed the good news to Madeleine and settled down to tell my story. After a couple of sentences into the story I noticed Madeleine was a bit distracted. Then she suddenly spoke,

"Has my mom ever told you that one day my brother drowned in our bathtub? The paramedics came with their tools but could not revive him. It took my parents a long time to get him back from heaven. My mom cried and cried and prayed to God for days and finally God sent him back." She stopped and kept looking at her teddy bear.

"Really?" I said in feigned surprise. "No, I haven't heard that horrible story." I looked at her. Avoiding my eyes, she kept holding her Teddy tightly. I realized that the story of Ganesh was no longer of interest to little Madeleine. Her head was now full of other important concerns. The good news of her little brother being out-of-danger was now replaced by an imaginary probability of his danger or even death. Her total rights to her parents' unconditional love for three years unexpectedly ended by the entry of her new brother. Indeed, this was a dangerously significant event for Madeleine. I looked at her and saw Madeleine deep in her thoughts, far away from me. A few minutes passed without any one of us saying anything. Then Madeleine came closer to my right ear and whispered,

"Do you know who came to Riki's funeral?" I shook my head.

"Our neighbor's black cat came with five other black cats. The six of them brought a golden box and put Riki's dead body in it and carried the box to heaven. Mom cried and cried. Dad was away in Japan."

"And you? Did you not cry?" I asked.

"No, not at all. I knew all along that Riki would not live because since birth he was very thin and weak." Madeleine stopped talking. Holding the bear tight in her arms, she pulled up the blanket to her chin and closed her eyes. Within a few minutes she fell asleep. I just could not bring myself to move her to her room.

Looking at the innocent beautiful face of a 5-year-old child I sat for a long time in stunning shock. What do we grown-ups know or understand about the mysterious depth of a child's imagination? That night Madeleine moved in her sleep quite a bit and I woke up every time she moved around. The next morning when Jacqueline returned home with Riki, Madeleine was still asleep in the guest room.

I never told Jacqueline about my conversation with Madeleine. Since that night Madeleine and I became close by a secret bond about which neither of us ever mentioned. I must say, looking back, I was quite impressed by her unique personality and the bizarre beauty of her imagination. Perhaps she would become a poet or a writer.

Eventually our lives took us in separate ways. The two families moved to different cities. But we kept in touch with occasional phone calls and Christmas cards.

Years later in one Christmas card Jacqueline scribbled that Madeleine finished medical school and was now doing her residency. I was reminded of our night together and wondered after all these years if Madeleine remembered her conversation with me that evening.

The Yellow Nursery

"Come to the homecoming party for my baby tomorrow afternoon, around four." Adele's voice beamed from the other end of the telephone.

"What baby? I didn't know you already found a child! Congratulations! I thought the process takes a couple of years." I said without thinking. We all knew about many trips Adele made to various countries and various agencies in order to adopt a child.

"Oh, you don't know the whole story and I don't have time to go into that now. Let's say she kind o' dropped into my lap. Am I lucky or what! See you tomorrow. Oh, by the way, don't bring anything pink. I chose yellow for her nursery. Ciao." Adele hung up leaving me with my questions.

I had known Adele twenty-five years ago when we were both in college. After college we lost contact for about twenty years until I got this job teaching at Denver University. I had been married and divorced twice and for last five years have been enjoying the bliss of single life. One day a neighbor, while chatting about therapy, casually mentioned the name of her marriage counselor and I was awe-struck. A few questions made it clear that it was indeed my very old roommate Adele. When I called, Adele was delighted to hear from me.

"Great, I found you again. Where have you been? I'm glad you are here. We can go skiing together. I have nobody to talk to. Being a therapist I have to keep my mouth shut. You never know who knows whom. You know what I mean!"

We began to do things together. As usual, I had to listen to Adele's non-stop talking including her sexual escapades. 'Some things never change,' I told myself. The gist of her life over the last twenty years was so strange that I was not sure if she was making things up. Of course, Adele always had a penchant to be involved in things bizarre and exciting. In college we used to watch her with envy. Apparently, she was married to a local politician, who was twenty odd years older, and had moved to Washington D.C. She wanted a child badly. Their vigorous efforts resulted in a fatal heart attack for the poor man. Adele had no inkling that her husband had an ailing heart. He left quite a bit of money and she went back to school, got a certificate as a marriage counselor, and moved to Denver to start fresh.

"When my husband died, I realized that if I wanted a child, I should not wait too long. I was already in my early forties. You know I always had many male friends and three of them kindly agreed to give me a baby. However, it did not work." She paused to enquire why I never had children.

"It just didn't happen. And I'm too much of a chicken to have a child by myself." I said apologetically.

"To make a long story short," Adele continued, "after many failed attempts, I decided to adopt. But the red tape is unbelievable. I can't wait for ever. I'm forty-five. Now or never."

Every time we met, Adele gave me the update on her search for a child. At some point I commented about her obsession about this. She became serious suddenly and merely said, "Don't be so quick to make judgments. Someday you'll know." Watching her expression, I let it go.

When I arrived at Adele's that afternoon the front street was lined with cars. Inside loads of people were talking, laughing and eating finger food from small paper plates. There was an atmosphere of joy and celebration everywhere. I couldn't see Adele but saw a long table full of gifts in the hallway. I added mine – an allergy-proof teddy bear with a yellow ribbon around its neck. Following the crowd, I ended up in Adele's second bedroom, which obviously was made into a nursery. Adele was not exaggerating. Everything was yellow except a humidifier on the floor. Adele sat on a low armchair with a bundle of yellow blanket in her arms. Everyone was listening quietly as she talked.

"Thank you all for coming to share my joy and to welcome my beautiful daughter Sorele. Many of you are curious about how I found her. She is the gift of a teen-aged mother. When I heard that this girl was pregnant and considered an abortion, I begged her to carry the child through and give her to me." The baby moved inside the blanket. Adele rocked her a bit and continued,

"When I was a child, I discovered that I didn't have a father and my mother kept telling me how I was an unwanted child. I was constantly reminded that all her misfortune was created by my existence. I thought of running away but felt sorry for her. She had no one else besides me. The only good thing she did was to put me through school. The year I graduated from high school my mother died after a brief illness. At her deathbed she told me if I wanted to be happy I should never be with men and never have children. She left me enough money to give me my freedom and made me an orphan at the same time. I was determined to disobey her. But despite my wishes and efforts I could not achieve either of these goals! I came to see her last words as a curse. Today that curse is broken. Whether my mother is happy or not, I am." A few drops of tears rolled down her cheeks. She lowered her face and kissed her baby's tiny forehead.

I stood for awhile feeling ashamed of all my past judgments. Suddenly everything began to make sense. After a long time, I felt the old envy and a new love for her.

Foible

Passion

One autumn evening when Father Collins first saw her in an embrace of a young man in front of the church, she did not look more than sixteen or perhaps eighteen. He could not be sure.

The only contact the priest had with women outside his family were women connected to the congregation and the women who come for confessions. The congregation appeared to be a collective body even though the confessions of individual woman were full of personal information filled with anger, remorse and even pleasure. Not seeing their faces, he never associated the confessions to any particular person. After nearly a lifetime in this work at age seventy-nine Father Collins often wondered if the Lord had given the female sex more problems or they merely liked to talk more about them. But now, suddenly the priest was puzzled by his own problem.

It was a Sunday afternoon in September. The priest had gone back to the church to pray. He was in turmoil. He seemed to have difficulty concentrating in his prayers. After nearly two hours of failed efforts, he opened his eyes to the large figure of Christ above and saw the kind face looking down. For the first time this gentle face appeared to be that of a stranger's. The flickering light of tall candles creating a misty halo barely illuminated the sad face. The longer he stared at

Christ above him, the more remote He seemed. Loneliness, instead of love, enveloped him now so strongly that he burst out sobbing. The priest felt a dull pain in his chest. He pulled himself up, straightening his tall stooping body, and walked out of the church.

Outside the church door on the top step, Father Collins noticed the beautiful sunset that colored the western sky with a pinkish purple hue. The color had a hypnotic effect on him as if he were noticing the mystery of Nature's beauty for the first time. As he walked down the steps leaving the church, an uncontrollable pull made him look back. That was when he saw two young people in an embrace behind the left pillar halfway down the steps. The young man was totally absorbed in crushing his lips on the girl's mouth in a frenzy, as if afraid that time, like the rapidly changing colors of the sky, would run out. But what really struck the priest was the girl's face, which he could see clearly. Her tender young face caught the glow of the setting sun and presented an image of exquisite beauty that he was unable to escape. Her eyes opened and she saw the priest. She blushed in embarrassment. The priest too was embarrassed and turned to leave. But the moment before he turned away, he knew that something ineffable had passed between them – the two unconnected beings three generations apart. The priest's loneliness and heartache of a few minutes back disappeared, replaced by an intense pleasure.

Walking away from the young couple, Father Collins knew a kind of love that he had never experienced before. It was love for a blushing young girl of sixteen or eighteen. This realization brought an unprecedented joy and at the same time, fear. After a long stroll in the cool evening when the priest returned home, he found his dinner prepared by the housekeeper still warm on the stove. But he was not hungry. He changed into a simple robe and knelt in front of the little crucifix in his bedroom. When he closed his eyes, however, he saw only a blushing face with a pair of shy eyes. Contact with his God failed, and after a long attempt, he went to bed exhausted.

For several weeks the priest struggled to control his desire – the obsession to find her, to find her body near his own. One evening as he was taking a stroll along the river – his favorite place in town – the autumn chill ran through his body, bringing close the reality of the coming winter. Yet as he pulled his cassock around him, a fiery sensation between his thighs hit him with enormous force of pain and pleasure at the same time. He had to sit down on the grass to keep from collapsing. He wanted her. Not knowing how to go about it, he crouched there for a long time, until he began to shiver in the evening chill.

Father Collins returned home late. He went to bed and fell into a tortured sleep. He stopped going out much and found himself unable to concentrate on anything, even reading the Bible. He considered going to confession. But he couldn't bring himself to do so because he had not committed any sin. Most of all, the risk of losing the pleasure, albeit painful, was too big a sacrifice to bear. He indulged in frequent fantasies in which he made love to his young beloved, only to be followed by the suffering from the utter disappointment that she was not with him in the flesh. Thus, the priest began to live in a world of fantasy where pleasure was short lived.

Two months after the priest first saw the girl, one Sunday morning, he awoke with a fresh feeling of hope. He felt like a new person. The morning promised a warm day with the sun shining from a cloudless sky. He took delight in a long bath and dressed carefully. He had a hearty lunch. A short nap afterwards made him feel rested. He was pleased to see the sun still in the sky. The afternoon light reminded him of another afternoon when he had laid his eyes on his beloved for the first time. He dressed quickly and walked out. As he reached the church steps the western sky melted into a dark pink and he waited near the left pillar halfway down the steps. He was almost sure she would come.

The sun dropped down and disappeared casting a diffuse twilight all around. Father Collins lost track of time. The chill in the air brought the cruel realization that she would not come to their rendezvous. As he descended the steps, he argued with himself that she might be waiting for him in a warm place. He walked hurriedly toward the cafe not far from the church. His legs went numb from standing too long and would not go as fast as he wished. Like the quickly falling night, a dark depression began to wrap him around. By now he knew that he had also lost his God, who could have helped him soothe his tortured soul. Like a dog in a winter night looking for a shelter out of sheer instinct for survival, the priest moved toward a roadside cafe for a warm drink.

After a cup of Irish coffee, Father Collins went out into the night. On the street ahead of him walked a couple, their arms around each other's waist. In the fog the two figures appeared like one. The dim streetlights seemed to increase the darkness, and the priest felt he was walking in a dream world. As he drew near the figures, they passed under a streetlamp and he could see her face clearly. It was not the young woman of his fantasy. During the rest of the way back to his home he thought of nothing but the avenging God.

This new preoccupation about God's revenge took his mind away from his love for a while. As he pondered about his fate, he could see a clear connection between the course of events and his initial mistrust in God on that fateful September afternoon. Over the fifty years that Father Collins had dedicated himself to his God, he had also been protected against the passion that had now attacked him so virulently. Or, was his love for God only a distraction from this passion? The more he struggled for an answer, the angrier he felt. However, deep inside, he knew that this preoccupation of his about God's revenge was temporary. The need to have his beloved in flesh would return with double force. He also knew that he must delay this as long as possible. For that would be the end of him. He wished to hold his beloved in his arms only once before he left this world. But he was determined not to ask the Almighty for such a favor.

Meanwhile, the winter began in full force. The wind howled through the trees in Father Collins's garden dropping the last dead leaves. His desire for the girl remained the same although his image of her now changed to that of a loving and affectionate one who also loved him but didn't know how to find him. Together they were at a loss, bewildered. This fantasy took him into a world where he searched for her and she looked for him, but both knew the deep love and passion they felt for each other. This new twist of imagination made the priest a lot calmer.

One morning in the middle of December, Father Collins awoke feeling better than usual. He had a dream that *he was young again and was preparing for his wedding to his beloved. She looked exquisite, just like he remembered seeing her the first time.* A wedding in his dream was more than he could ask for. As he left his bed, he felt like lighting a candle in front of the crucifix for the first time in a long time. He decided to go out for a walk.

Walking absent-mindedly Father Collins found himself approaching his church. He went inside and sat on one of the back pews. There was no one in the church at this time of the day. For the first time in several months the priest began to pray and this time it was Christ whose face appeared in his mind. Christ's face looked kind but sad. Refracted through the stained-glass windows a few rays of red and blue light fell on the tall marble figure. The priest strained his eyes to look closely and saw tears on Christ's cheeks. He sat there praying for a long time. Tears began to roll down the priest's cheeks now. Father Collins knelt to pray in gratitude.

The caretaker of the church found the priest on the floor between two pews that evening. He had a peaceful death, the doctor said.

A Day of a Therapist's Practice

(A satirical one act play)

[Dr Bruce Edelstein, a Jungian psychotherapist walks in with a briefcase bulging with files. He has an inexpensive suit on, and a tie that is off-center under the collar of a faded shirt and a cap on his head. He takes the cap off, hangs it on a peg, takes the coat off, puts it behind the chair and drops the file at the foot of the chair after taking out a yellow pad and a pen. He places a box of Kleenex on the table near the second chair facing him. He sits on the one with extra padding, looks at his watch and stretches his legs on the table. A knock on the door makes him sit up and take his legs down. Quickly he straightens his tie, moves his hand briefly over his balding head.]

Dr E : Come in!

[An intense-looking woman around 50 enters. She is dressed in a long skirt and heels with a couple of colorful silk scarves hanging over a cotton blouse.]

Dr E : Miss Sullivan? Please [pointing to the only other chair across the table. Mary Sullivan sits, then gets up, looks around and moves the chair toward the analyst a bit and sits, smoothes her skirt, rearranges her scarves, crosses her legs – uncrosses again and looks at the analyst and the wall behind him, smiles briefly before changing into a serious face again. All this takes up a couple of minutes.]

Dr E : I'm Dr Bruce Edelstein, [extending his hand, which Mary takes and shakes strongly making a slight bowing gesture still saying nothing. Dr E clears his throat a little and speaks, looking at her directly.] How may I help you?

Mary S : Well, I really don't know what to say. You see, I looked you up on the Internet, I mean all of you guys – the Jungians in the area. I picked your name… your name sounds like a real psychoanalyst. I've had therapy off and on for many years. First in California where my ex-boyfriend lived, and I lived with him for couple of years. I was in my twenties. It was about my tendency to find abusive men. Then I had therapy in New York for five years because I could not attract anyone. The long story short, my best friend Sharon told me recently that I need to see a Jungian. Sharon, you see, has vast experience in therapy. She even had two years of training in counseling. [Dr E looked distracted and a bit impatient moving his chair with some noise trying to avoid looking at the clock on the wall. Mary continues.] Anyway, Sharon tells me that a Jungian therapist can help me with my soul. What is soul work anyway?

Dr E : [Ignoring the last question] What do <u>you</u> think is your problem? Why did you want to see me or anyone else?

Mary S : I'm not sure. Sharon thinks I need to settle down, have a family. I'm fifty-three. It's a bit late for that, don't you think? I mean - to have my own children. All these years I haven't managed to find a husband either. I have a good income and a few good friends. Sharon is one of them. We go to the movies and restaurants and have fun. I guess I could adopt a child, but frankly I'm scared to take care of a baby. I think I'm fine and don't miss not having a man in the house. I can have sex whenever I want. You see in my job that's not a problem.

Dr E : [Nervously] What is your job?

Mary S : Oh, I do erotic massage. I'm trained as a massage therapist. We help our clients relax, help them with all kinds of problems from muscle pains to sexual malfunction. [She smiles with a wink.]

Dr E: I see. [Distraught, he looks away and looks back at her again, moves in his chair a bit appearing both curious and embarrassed. A silence fell between them for a minute or so.] I – I still don't see what exactly is your problem or how I can help you.

Mary S : Well, I'm okay most of the time. Sometimes, when I can't fall asleep, I worry. I'm not sure I should be doing this line of work. Although I have to say I enjoy my job most of the time. It pays so well, and my clients are happier when they leave my office. But I'm not so sure anymore. The other day, there was this cute guy – in his twenties – he had a body like one of those models in fashion magazines. As I was massaging him, he had this big [shows a size with her two hands. Dr E interrupts her before she finishes the sentence.]

Dr E : Look Miss Sullivan, I really don't need to hear the details of this man's physiology. I'm still trying to understand why you're here wasting my time and your money. [He sounds slightly annoyed this time.]

Mary S : Well, I'm trying to tell you. You keep interrupting me. Everything went well with this guy, but then one thing led to another, and we had sex. He doubled my fee, he was so happy. Afterwards when I went out with my girlfriends, Sharon asked me if we had protection. I got a shock and kept worrying about all kinds of things – AIDS and other horrible things. Usually, I don't go that far. He was so cute and eager and paid a bunch in advance. [Dr E looks a bit relaxed and more attentive. She pauses for a few seconds before continuing.] Since then, I have been questioning my line of work, my life. I'm really scared. [She appears quite upset and looks away fixing her stare on the wall behind the analyst.]
Dr E : So, you're no longer as happy with your work as you were before – you're suffering from some guilt, – eh, eh some second thoughts, right?
Mary S : No, not really. Yes, some guilt for not using protection. I'm just afraid what may happen. But I like my work. I make a bundle and I enjoy myself. I have no intention of giving it up. I put away over forty thousand grand a year for my retirement. No other job will offer me that kind of money. [Dr E looks surprised and a bit jealous perhaps.]
Dr E : Wow, that's – that's good saving. Well, have you considered doing the same work without the sexual part? There are many massage therapists in this town. I hear they charge 80 to 100 dollars an hour and make good living.
Mary S. : That's out of question. The competition among regular massage therapists is tough. Besides, I have a reputation to maintain. [Looking at him directly] If you don't believe me

try me once. I'll give you a free session. Better still, we can swap this session. I guarantee you, you'll come out feeling a lot better than I will after this hour, I bet you.

Dr E : [Smiling] Thanks, but no thanks. I cannot do that. It would be unethical. By the way, coming to see me does not guarantee 'feeling good.' It guarantees nothing. But if you cooperate, eventually you may feel more satisfied with your life and may even feel less guilty. I can't assure you that you haven't contacted HIV/AIDS or any other sexually transmitted disease. You need to go see a primary care doctor for that. But you'll have to wait at least three months before they can test you. I can give you a few names of internal medicine doctors, if you want. Meanwhile, you need to understand why you're in this kind of work. Together we may figure out the purpose and meaning of your lifestyle and that may help.

Mary S : Tell me doctor why should I pay you by the hour just to find out why I feel guilty. I already know that. Sharon tries to convince me that I need to do soul work. What is soul work anyway? I really would like to know.

Dr E : Well, it's hard to explain. If you keep coming, and together we look at your dreams, talk about your life – you begin to know about yourself in a deeper way. You see, there is always more to us – a deeper side, [moving his right palm from his chest to the belly to indicate the depth] which is unknown to us, and which really guides our actions. We call it the unconscious, what the public calls sub-conscious. Your soul is actually that unknown part of you that I can help you to open up and make available.

Mary S : [Listening intently] Wow, that sounds like deep stuff. I can't say I understand everything you said. You mentioned dreams. Sharon told me that you Jungians like dreams. So, I scribbled down my dream from last night. Do you want to hear it?

Dr E : Yes, yes. Thank you. That would be splendid. Now we're getting somewhere. [He moves forward in his chair with new enthusiasm.]

Mary S : [Looks for the dream in her handbag, inside a date book, even inside her wallet.] Well, I seem to have misplaced the piece of paper. But I remember it. It's quite brief. I dreamed of the young man I mentioned to you earlier. We were in bed making love. It was so vivid that I woke up feeling his presence right on my bed. It felt wonderful.

Dr E : [Visibly uncomfortable] Miss Sullivan, this dream sounds like a real wish-fulfilling thing. Are you sure you have dreamed it? Do you want a continuing relationship with this young man?

Mary S : You bet I do. But I can't. I'm a professional. I have already gone too far. God knows I may have to pay heavily for my action. But I can't get him out of my system; you know what I mean.

Dr E [Looking at the clock] I'm sorry our time is up. We can make another appointment if you want. My fee is 250 dollars please.

Mary S : Let me think about it. I'll call you. I'm scheduled to see a few other therapists in next few days. As for the fee, here is my card. Call me if you change your mind about swapping the hour. If not, I'll send you a check by mail. I don't carry my checkbook, unless you take credit cards – Visa, American Express, Capital One, whatever. I have them all.

Dr E : [Slightly annoyed] Please send me the check. Here is my card with the address. Remember it's 250 dollars.

[Mary Sullivan gathers her handbag and leaves with a brief 'bye now.' After she leaves, Dr Edelstein picks up the card she has left on the table, looks at it and puts it in his briefcase. He gets up from his chair, stretches a bit, shakes his head to himself and speaks aloud.] Forty thousand a year! Unbelievable! I'm in the wrong profession.

[A knock. Dr E adjusts his tie and moves his hand over his balding head automatically. A middle-aged man – dressed casually – enters. He seems at ease and comes forward to shake Dr E's hand, introduces himself as Terence Parsons, sits on the second chair and smiles.]

Dr E : Hello. What brings you here today?

T P : See Dr Edelstein, I heard that you Jungians are different. Perhaps, you can help me. I have this authority complex – I guess. I have changed jobs many times in my life. I'm terrified to face my bosses. I even considered starting a business of my own, but I don't have that kind of money. My wife has some money that she inherited from a rich aunt. But she is not willing to invest in business. She likes Mutual Funds. At any rate, 10 years ago I went to an old-fashioned Freudian – recommended by my father-in-law – and laid on a couch five times a week trying my damdest to recall if I really wanted to kill my father as a child or wanted to sleep with my mother.

The only thing I remembered was the football coach, who asked me to take my pants off when I was in 7th grade. But this information did not seem to interest my analyst that much.
[He stops for a second and Dr E takes the opportunity to speak.]
Dr E : Has anything happened then, I mean with the coach?
T P : [Ignoring the question] After three years of my Freudian analysis and a lot of dollars I was so frustrated that I went to a Gestalt therapist, a woman – that my wife got the name from a woman friend. Apparently only a few of her kind of therapist left on this coast. They have all gathered in California or moved to Holland. [Dr E tries to look at his wristwatch with the corner of his eye. He moves in his chair showing slight impatience. Unaware of his listener's reactions the patient continues.] With the Gestalt analyst I tried to act like whatever appeared in my dreams – a river, a turkey or the lady next door. In 11 months, I became pretty good at this acting thing, but my problems remained as before. I sweated every time my boss summoned me in his office for no apparent reason. I was terrified. Of course, with the Gestalt lady I paid a lot less. Then a friend suggested Rolfing. He said it changed his life. Boy, I had no idea what I was in for. [The patient gets up from his chair and gesticulates as he speaks.] My body hurt so bad that I screamed in sheer pain. I was told that I was breaking through my inhibitions. I felt okay after a week or so when my muscles healed and got used to the method. I began to look forward to my Rolfing sessions. But I still sweated every time my boss called or I ran into him.

[Dr E suppressed a yawn, visibly bored but kept a smile on his face trying to look attentive. The patient paused briefly and began again.] Then a colleague told me about a retreat in California in Big Sur, beautiful spot. Cost me a bundle, some kind of Oriental thing. Zen Western style or some such name, I can't remember now. For a whole weekend I sat on my rear end and tried to meditate. It was a cliff above the Pacific Ocean, but I couldn't even enjoy the view because I had to keep my eyes closed all the time. In the end I got very angry and caught a bad cold from the sea breeze that blew pretty hard. After a week of tofu and bean sprouts I flew back. The only good thing was that I lost five pounds.

Dr E : [Interrupting] When did all this happen? Is there any reason for me to know all this?

T P : [A little embarrassed] Well, I thought you'd like to know my history and how I got here. It's my nephew Ron who suggested that I try a Jungian. By the way, Ron had applied to the Jung Institute of Boston and was rejected. But he may apply again. The letter of rejection was fairly encouraging – 'not at this time, maybe later' something like that. He has the same last name. Ronald Parsons. In case…

Dr E : I have nothing to do with the Jung Institute. I used to be quite involved, but not anymore. So I can't help your nephew. Back to your problem. Could you describe to me exactly what happens when you meet your boss?

T P : As I said, I sweat, I begin to feel hot and shaky even when I think about such an encounter.

Dr E : Does this happen with any other person?

T P : Now that you ask, yes. On rare occasions I have similar symptoms with my wife, especially if she is being – you know – bossy. By the way my wife doesn't think it's a big deal except she complains about the laundry bill. You know the sweating and all. I was wondering if you could tell me what really is at the bottom of it. What is my real problem, doctor?

Dr E [Visibly annoyed looks at his watch, moves on his chair, sits up and talks.] You really want to know? You are a compulsive talker – that's your problem. A verbal compulsion and the treatment of such problems takes time. You may also have a hyperactive sweat gland. I need to know more about the triggering situations. [Terence Parsons is about to say something, but Dr E gestures him to stop. However, the patient bursts out.]

T P : How is that possible? My wife always complains that I don't talk to her. I thought all these years of therapy cured me of at least that problem. Now I'm totally confused. [He looks distraught, moves in his chair, and moves his arms in a way as if he has begun to sweat. He takes out a checkbook, writes a check quickly and puts it in front of the analyst. He gets up.] I think I shall leave. Thanks for your time doctor. Goodbye.

Dr E : What about the next appointment? [Terence Parsons is already out of the door.]

Dr Edelstein takes a deep breath, looks at the watch and sighs deeply. : What a day! At this rate I shall never make a living. Well, at least one is coming back for the second hour. [He wipes his neck and face with a handkerchief that he pulls out of his shirt pocket. He quickly fixes things, looks at the appointment book and checks the name. A knock.] Come in, come in please!

[A woman in her late 30s or early 40s in a short tight skirt and a sleeveless top enters and he shakes her hand and smiles in recognition. She takes the chair and pulls it a bit closer to his. She opens her handbag, takes out a small mirror, fixes her hair and smiles seductively and crosses her legs. In addition to heavy make-up, she has several strings of glass beads around the neck and long earrings nearly touching her shoulders.]

Dr E :Well, how are you today, Miss Brown?

Miss B. : I'm sort of okay Dr. Einstein, I wanted to ask you something.

Dr E : It's Dr. Edelstein. I don't dare to be mistaken for the great man.

Miss B. : Oh, I'm sorry, Dr. Edelweiss, whatever. Why don't I call you Dr E or Bruce? That's a lot easier. You can call me Molly, although I prefer my middle name, which is Abigail after my mother's great-aunt. Mum's family was all originally Yankee. Apparently, Abigail's grandfather and grandmother had met on the boat – the Mayflower – and never got married. So I'm a child born of original sin. [Laughs aloud.] Here I'm telling you all my deep dark secrets, but you… [trails off]

Dr E : Miss Brown, Molly eh. Abigail, how can I help you?

Miss B: Well, I was talking to my girlfriend about you, us. She told me that the therapy is really warming up. She should know. She has been a trainee for ten years at a Jung Institute out West somewhere. When I told her about you, she said something about a 'transfer' or something like that. What does she mean Dr E?

Dr E. [Looking uncomfortable] : Well, it may not be a good idea to talk to your girlfriend about us – about our sessions. This work needs privacy … secrecy… eh… [stops after noticing her expression, which is happy.]

Miss B : I get it. It's our secret. [She looks at Dr E seductively.]

Dr E : [Desperate to change the subject] Have you had a dream to talk about?

Miss B : Oh yes, yes. I tried to type it as you said. But you see I don't have a computer and my neighbor's is on the blink right now. Anyway, I wrote it down longhand. Next time I'll make you a copy, okay? [She begins to look inside her handbag, takes out a few items – lipstick, wallet, small mirror, car-keys – puts them on the table and looks inside, then puts everything back again. She gets up puts her hand inside her jacket pocket.] Gee, I thought I might have put it right here [putting her hand inside her blouse. Unsuccessful she looks inside her wallet again and pulls out a long strip of paper like a grocery bill. She stretches it out and with a smile] Here we are.

Dr E : [Increasingly getting annoyed with her but trying to hide the feeling with a fake smile] You call it longhand? Looks like shorthand to me.

Miss B : Well, most of it is in my head anyway. I shall never forget this dream. I just jotted some vital points, you see. I learned this technique in college, how to write only a few critical words of a lecture and later I could make total recall.

[Dr E waits with expectation.]
Miss B : [Looks at the piece of paper, crumbles it in her palm, moves forward in her chair and looks at the analyst directly] 'We are – you and I – in a restaurant. You take my coat and lead me to a table. It's a nice cozy restaurant and we sit opposite each other. You order two glasses of white wine. When we're served you raise your glass and make a toast to us. The waiter comes and you order a clam chowder and I order a steak – rare. The waiter brings a bottle of red wine, and you keep pouring it in my glass. I drink and drink. Soon everything becomes blurry.' [At this point she closes her eyes. The analyst is fidgety in his chair. Miss B continues with her eyes closed] 'Your face changes into Steve's – my first lover – then you change into Gary, the guy I'd met in New York and spent a night with and then'... [Dr E interrupts]
Dr E : [Without hiding his annoyance] Miss, Miss Brown...
Miss B : Molly, although I prefer Abigail. You know my great-aunt came from some place in Northern England and...
Dr E : [Determined to interrupt] No, I don't know and I don't care. Please let's get back to the dream. Shall we? Let's stay with the dream symbols.
Miss B : I'm sorry. My other analyst wanted me to say anything that came to my mind when I told him my dreams. You see, I have vivid imagination. I like to dance around a word, and it comes naturally to me. But if you want me to shut up, I will. I can do it.
Dr E : No, no. Please don't shut up. But I thought you wanted to understand your dream. We Jungians believe that free

association – saying anything that comes to your mind – takes you away from your eh … eh … never mind. Let me ask you this. Are you sure this was really your dream?

Miss B : Oh yes, it was my dream alright. Should I stop or continue? I haven't even gotten to the most exciting part.

Dr E : [Alarmed] Let's pause for a moment and look at what we have here. You have to realize that a dream must be understood as a symbolic message from the unconscious. [Ignoring her puzzled look] We need to look at each symbol at a time and see what it may mean. For example, what is a restaurant to you?

Miss B [Looks relaxed again and giggles a bit] A restaurant? For me? I go there to eat. Men take me there and they usually pay. No wait a minute. A guy I once met in the mall took me out and did not pay for me, only his part. He didn't tell me that we were going Dutch. I thought it was rude, don't you?

Dr E : [Without responding to her question] So you go to a restaurant to eat with men. Eating, you see, is essential for our bodies. It's nutrition.

Miss B : [Jumping in] Oh yes, I once knew a woman who was a nutritionist in a hospital. She always measured calories before she ate anything. Then at age 50 she began to gain weight and in a few months she swelled up like a balloon. I kid you not. She was this fat [showing with her two hands.]

Dr E : Miss Brown – Molly, could we stay with the dream, please? [He looks at his watch] We don't have much time left. I want you to know that the fact that you have dreamed of me does not mean it's me. Remember, I change into other men?

I can easily be an inner figure, who appears in many shapes and forms.

Miss B : [Looking totally confused] I don't understand. I swear it was you. You were wearing the shirt just like this one, you had no hair, even your glasses looked the same. How could it not be you? Now you really got to me. Are you saying you're embarrassed that you took me to the restaurant? Gee, Nancy never told me that Jungians talk in riddles. [She takes out her check book looking visibly disappointed.]

Dr E : [Taking out his appointment book] Let's see, can you come a little later next week? I have to teach a class and I won't be free until...

Miss B : [Interrupting] I don't know if I can make it next week. [She finishes writing the check and leaves it on the table.] I'll call you. [She gathers her things and leaves in a hurry ignoring the analyst's stretched hand to shake.

[Dr. Bruce Edelstein picks up the check, examines it, drops it in his briefcase. He stretches and talks to himself.] What a day! My ex-wife was right. I should have stayed with the hospital and just kept writing prescriptions for the anti-depressants. No one wants deep analysis.

Martinis and Chocolate Mousse

"Sweetheart, I'm going out for a few minutes. Need to pick up something. Do answer the phone, please. Be back in a jiffy." Rebecca runs out of the kitchen as Peter keeps his eyes on the Sunday New York Times. Peter has a hard time shifting his attention from the President's speech on the economy to his wife's parting message. She said something about the phone.

Of course, he will answer the phone. Is she expecting one of the kids to call? They do call on Sundays. But then, they call any day when they need something, especially money. How he wishes the phone will not ring for at least one hour until Rebecca gets back. Why don't people call her cell number? Isn't that customary nowadays? Most of their close friends know that Peter does not like talking on the phone and that he doesn't bother with social niceties at all.

Would they have so many friends at their age if Rebecca did not make a point of keeping in touch with everybody? Peter wonders. The dinner party that evening, for example, is one of the ways his wife keeps in touch with their circle of friends and colleagues. Peter knows that Rebecca will be depressed unless she throws at least one party a month if not two. For him these parties are nothing but unnecessary distractions and a waste of money. God knows, he does not need them.

He seems to be distracted most of the time anyway. If only the world, Rebecca, children and friends would leave him alone this one day of the week, so he is free to read the Sunday paper in peace and do nothing else all day!

Actually, Rebecca does not bother him until party-time when, as usual, he is expected to fix drinks, pour wine during dinner and make coffee afterwards. He doesn't mind that so much and is willing to go along with one party a month for her sake. She loves giving parties – to plan, to shop, to cook, to dress up, being charming all evening and even bubbly afterwards when the two of them clean up.

It was at a party that they had met twenty-seven years ago. He hadn't been able to keep his eyes off her that evening. Even her name sounded the loveliest he had ever heard. Rebecca Wilson. Perhaps that's the reason he could never use a nick name like Becky to call his wife. Could he possibly give her his name? How nice it would sound! Rebecca O'Conner. Mrs. Rebecca O'Conner. He never imagined anyone could be so vibrant. That infectious liveliness! By the end of the evening, he was determined to be close to Rebecca Wilson. Somehow, he knew that being near her would make life worth living. Yet after almost three decades of this most desirable life together, why everything had paled so much, Peter could not help wondering.

He is shocked out of his reverie when the phone rings. By the time he gathers the scattered newspaper and gets to the phone, it has stopped ringing. He just cannot move so fast anymore. He never really could, compared to other people. But Rebecca never slows down. At sixty she is still her same perky self, attending to whatever needs or does not need her attention.

What is taking her so long? She ought to be here to answer the phone. She loves talking on the phone, something he quite dislikes. Someone somewhere said that differences like these made marriages more successful! How the hell do they know?

Rebecca walks in with two grocery bags in her arms, letting the screen door slam behind her. Peter winces at the harsh bang.

"Any calls? They don't have fresh mussels. I have to think of something else for the first course."

"Steamed mussels. Ah! They are good. No, no calls. Can't you use clams instead?"

"I guess I could. Didn't think of that. Got some avocados and shrimp instead. You don't mind, do you?"

"Me? Of course, not. Anything you make is always good. Besides, I'm not your guest."

"You are. When I plan a meal for others I always think of you – what you like. Don't tell anyone that though." Rebecca winks. "Remember when we were in Spain? You liked the paella in that restaurant in Barcelona so much that I had to flirt with the chef to get the recipe. You were even..." The shrill ring of the telephone interrupts her.

"I'm upstairs, if you need me." Showing no sign of having heard the paella story, Peter walks toward the stairs with the bundle of New York Times. He sits in his study looking out the window. A chipmunk scurries up the big maple tree in the backyard. How hard they had argued, he and Rebecca, whether to cut the tree down to allow more sun into the vegetable patch. That was the first year of their move to this house. Now, they hardly notice how much sun the tree really obstructs. Rebecca is no longer that interested in gardening. As he recalls he had been against cutting the maple down. The chipmunk runs after something and disappears. Peter sits a few minutes longer feeling very lazy. Is he becoming like his father already? The old man had become a hermit in his sixties and disappeared from sight when Peter's mother had company. Oh, well, it isn't really Rebecca's fault. The party, which was planned a month ahead, had to be shifted to Sunday. He has had a faculty meeting on Saturday evening. He looks at his watch.

Two more hours to go before the guests – Rebecca's guests - are due to arrive. No, that's not quite fair. His buddy John from the History Department will be here too. He needs to get ready. Rebecca will be upset if he's not ready when she comes up to dress. He avoids looking closely into the mirror as he shaves rapidly. The warm shower does not help lift his spirits. Hopefully the martinis will. Nowadays the only aspect of these parties he looks forward to is the alcohol.

As he rummages through the stack of ties, he cannot find the one he wants to wear with the shirt he has just put on. Why the hell does he need to wear a matching tie anyway? Well, he doesn't have to wear this shirt either, though Rebecca likes it and always comments how good he looks in it. If he wears a sports shirt with open collar, he hardly needs a tie. He suddenly thinks of his safari suit, which is tucked away on the overhead shelf of the closet. Of course, Rebecca likes him to dress properly for a dinner party. She did not like the safari suit when he bought it on impulse two summers ago. Why is suddenly every decision becoming a dilemma?

He is still standing in front of his closet when Rebecca rushes by him into the bathroom.

"Honey, please hurry," she says, "One of us ought to be down. They'll start arriving in a sec." Peter makes up his mind to wear the safari suit and dresses hurriedly, humming a tune the words of which he cannot remember. He is behind the counter in the kitchen fixing a stiff drink for himself when the doorbell rings.

"Hi there. Good to see you, John. Please make yourselves comfortable. Rebecca will be down shortly. John, the usual? What would you like?" he asks John's new and second wife, whose name Peter always forgets.

"I'll get it Peter. I know exactly what Nicole likes. Yeah, the usual for me." John says. Ever since John married this graduate student two years before, Peter has had a hard time thinking of her as John's wife. He was quite fond of Barbara, John's wife of many years. Rebecca, on the other hand, seems to have no trouble incorporating Nicole into their middle-aged group. Though she does mention occasionally how strangely Nicole dresses. Peter wishes he was as generous! Why is he unable to accept Nicole as his best friend's wife? Is it because of a secret wish that Peter cannot admit even to himself? He's jealous of John who had the guts to get out of an old marriage and find this beautiful young body to enjoy in his bed.

Rebecca walks in, radiant in her salmon-pink satin blouse and long black skirt. Peter looks up and wonders how on earth she manages to be so upbeat all the time!

"Darling, get me a sherry, please." Rebecca walks fast toward the front door where the rest of the guests begin to arrive. Peter feels a touch of heat around his earlobes. Why an innocent request from the woman he loves, suddenly sounds like an order! He spills some sherry as he pours a glass for his wife. Everyone except Peter and John follows Rebecca to the living room. John looks at Peter for a few seconds before asking, "What's up old buddy?" So, John has noticed that he's not in a party mood. Peter pours more vodka into his glass of dwindling Martini and looks at John without saying anything.

"Peter, could you bring the dish of cashews when you come, please?" Rebecca calls from the living room.

"Let's join them," says Peter, arranging various drinks on a tray forgetting the dish of cashews.

"Hey, that's a smart suit you've got, Peter. I didn't know you guys were in Africa." Bob Marshall of the department of Medieval Art History laughs as if he has just cut the greatest joke of the evening. No one except his wife Helen manages a giggle. For the first time Rebecca notices what Peter is wearing.

"You forgot the cashews, dear," Rebecca says and adds under her breath, "Must you always?"

Is she referring to the safari suit or the cashews? Peter keeps wondering as he gulps his double Martini. His wife goes back to the kitchen for the bowl of cashews.

Halfway through the dinner, the conversation begins to split up among pairs. Rebecca and Bob, John and Helen, Peter and Nicole. It has to be Rebecca's idea to put Peter and Nicole next to each other. He knows he ought to be polite. But what does one say to a new wife of a friend who is neither one's wife's nor one's daughter's age? If only the dinner would not drag on and on.

"Nicole, how do you like your new job?" Rebecca threw in from the other end of the table. Annoyed by the realization that Rebecca noticed his problem, Peter concentrates on finishing his chocolate mousse, desperately keeping his eyes on the dish. "Don't you like the mousse tonight, darling?" Rebecca threw in from the other end again as she shows signs of getting up from her chair. Peter does not bother to make a response.

Rebecca and Helen begin to stack the dishes in the kitchen and the men gravitate toward the living room. Peter looks up to see Nicole's bare neck. She is looking at the watercolor above the sideboard. He swallows the last of his chocolate mousse and gets up.

"Darling, four coffees and two teas, please. Do you need any help?" Rebecca calls from the kitchen. Peter runs upstairs. He makes it to the bathroom and closes the door. As he splashes cold water on his face after he throws up, he cannot avoid looking at the mirror this time. The tired and desperate face of an aging man stares back. He is tired, very tired. He closes the bedroom door behind him and collapses on their king-size-bed, closing his eyes.

If only he could get away from it all! The soft curve of a bare neck floats into his consciousness. He can almost feel the taut skin that is young and full of promise. How he would have loved to touch that skin once. Perhaps more than once and go further. For the first time Peter allows himself to indulge into a full erotic fantasy with the young body of a woman who is married to his best friend.

"Peter, are you alright?" A knock followed by John's voice cuts into his fantasy. He was about to hold Nicole's body in his arms. Her husband interrupts! In spite of himself the comic irony makes Peter smile. He opens his eyes. Instantly the alluring curves of a naked body disappear. Peter stretches over Rebecca's side of the bed reluctantly, and pulls himself up. The familiar smell of his wife's night cream on her pillow brings him back to his everyday reality that is inescapable and Peter knows that. Somehow he manages to stand up and opens the door.

"I'm fine; just resting a bit. Let's go down and join the others," he manages to avoid John's eyes the rest of the evening.

Alone

Sherry's Challenge

Sherry was turning the pages of an old *TIME* magazine in the waiting room of the X-ray/Imaging section of the hospital. She was a bit cold in the hospital cotton robe that was clean but not ironed. She had just had her routine mammogram for the second time and was waiting for the okay from the radiologist. She wasn't worried, although a faint needle of anxiety scraped some part of her consciousness gently. What's taking the doctor so long? "If the pictures don't come out right, whose fault is it," she wondered, "the machine, the tech, or the doctor who reads the X-ray images?"

"Mrs. Kimble? Hi, I'm Dr. Parker. Could you please come with me?" Trying not to worry, she followed the doctor, a petite woman in her forties in a white coat, to a small office and sat opposite her, a desk with papers and a computer between them. Dr. Parker got up and pointed to a set of large negatives hung on the wall and showed some gray dots with a pointer saying,

"These patches here are a bit suspicious. We need to make sure these are nothing serious. So I suggest a needle biopsy which can be done right away or you may come back tomorrow if you prefer. I already contacted the surgeon on duty. Would you like to contact your husband or anyone at home? It'd take another hour or so."

"Let's do it today. I have time now, tomorrow is not good. My husband is away on a business trip. I'm fine, so far anyway." She tried to sound casual.

Two days later when the doctor called with the positive biopsy result, Sherry was in total shock. Despite all her anxieties she never thought she would add to the national statistics of one of eight women. Some merciful natural defense kept her from the thought of impending suffering and death. She became busy dealing with the practical side of the news. She decided not to call her husband or her children with the news yet. 'Let them enjoy doing what they're doing for now. They'll know soon enough.' For once, she was alone to take care of herself. She met with several doctors – surgeons, oncologists, radiotherapists. The decision was to operate on the tumor and make a definitive diagnosis before the treatment plans could be made.

Two days later she got herself admitted for a lumpectomy. Just before the anesthesia took effect she had a sudden burst of tears flooding her face, robe and bed. For the first time she was hit by the severity of the situation. She was alone facing a serious health crisis that might end in death. Yet, for the first time Sherry also felt tender and loving toward this woman who was now lying on a hospital bed waiting for a surgeon's knife in her breast. The same breasts that she so carefully adorned with expensive bras and fitting tops to attract attention; the same breasts which gave pleasures to her lovers and herself; the same breasts that gave life nourishing milk to her two children. Her breasts had been such integral parts of herself, her identity. The nurse rubbed her arm saying,

"Don't be nervous. You won't feel a thing. It'd be over before you know it." The surgeon walked in and introduced himself, sat next to her bed and took her palm in his and said,

"It's okay to cry. Crying is good." Sherry wanted to hug the elderly man who understood her more than the woman nurse did.

The night after the lumpectomy, Sherry had the following brief dream.

"*She is in a hospital surrounded by doctors. Something profound is going to happen, but she does not know what. A nurse gives her a shot and two men in uniform push her bed toward the operating room. On the way, she sees a row of women. She recognizes her great grandmother, her grandmother, her mother and her two sisters, all lined up praying for her.*" Sherry awoke from the dream with a great sense of peace and security. Later, she knew that this dream helped her recovery more than anything.

The surgery revealed that no lymph nodes were involved and cancer was localized in a small tumor that was taken out followed by several weeks of radiation therapy. Sherry made friends with the whole team of doctors, technicians and nurses. She looked forward to her daily visits for radiation treatment.

Sherry didn't join any support group that the doctors recommended. She continued living her life as before and kept to herself. During this time, she knew her life had shifted to a level that she could not comprehend. Cancer brought a gift that she didn't know was possible. She began to take herself seriously and love herself deeply.

Saturday Evening

Wife - Do we have to go? I was so looking forward to a quiet evening for a change.

Husband - We said yes a month back. They're our closest friends. It doesn't look good to back off now over some lame excuse, don't you think? What is your excuse anyway?

Wife - Why is it that I'm not allowed to change my mind just because we said yes once. If they are real friends, they'll understand. Besides we aren't the only guests. There are others.

Husband - It's a matter of spending three hours with close friends. Since when you are so reluctant to party?

Wife - Since now. I have decided to live by my feelings from now on. All my life I have tried to please everyone except me. I'm entitled to be myself for a change. I shall call them and explain. Besides, I'm tired of spending a whole evening gossiping about other friends and eating and drinking until we cannot move any more. Sorry, you'll have to go without me this time.

Husband - What will you do home alone on a Saturday evening?

Wife - Nothing. No, I take it back. I think I'll draw a bath with lavender oil you gave me for my birthday and soak in that divine fragrance and read Tony Morrison. I need a warm soak to moisten her terse style. Have you noticed we never have time to read? All our evenings and weekends disappear between CNN and going out.

Husband - If you feel this way, I can't force you. You better call them and give a damn good excuse. Soaking in the tub may not convince them. I shall go and, please don't use this to call me selfish in the future.

Wife - I already told you to go without me. I shall call Julie and tell her the truth. She'll understand.

Husband - Good luck! What's going on Sherry? I mean really?

Wife - I'm not sure. Last few days I've been feeling kind of restless, as if I'm missing something. Something is passing me by. This afternoon as I was driving home, it hit me at the crossing of Weber and Maple that actually *it's me* who is passing me by. Do you know what I'm saying?

Husband - No.

Wife - I suppose I'm bored, bored with myself. It has nothing to do with you or anyone else. Well, don't you have to get ready? Could you do me a favor Honey? Please don't apologize for me. Give them my love.

Husband - After twenty-six years of marriage, I have to admit I still cannot make you out. Enjoy your bath. I hope the lavender oil is good enough to soften Tony Morrison's prose.

Wife - Go, get going. You'd be late. Don't come back early for my sake. Bye.

(Soaking her body fully in the warm water with her eyes closed)
Wife - Ah, what a pleasure! I need to do this more often.

A Break

The little piece of paper is stuck under the coffee mug. This is the mug Jonathan uses every morning to drink his coffee. It was a gift from their oldest daughter Megan for his forty-fifth birthday last year. A simple line design of a face on the mug is staring at his wife now. A half-moon-face with droopy eyes as if Mr. Moon-face just woke up. That was the idea. Jonathan always says that he cannot open his eyes without his first sip of coffee. Janet, his wife wonders what the scrap of paper may be saying and casually picks up the note still thinking it's just a piece of paper that got stuck under the mug. The moon-faced sleepy head! No, it looks like Jonathan's handwriting. Maybe he had to go somewhere early. But this is Saturday!

Janet switches on the automatic coffee-maker before looking at the note. It reads,

"I'm leaving. Forgive me for not preparing you for this. I need to be alone. I need to think about us, about my work – about everything. I'm tired, tired of everything and cannot take it any longer. I shall be in touch when I'm ready. Tell the kids whatever you like. I'm not trying to be dramatic. On the contrary, I thought a great deal before writing this note. This seems the best way. Forgive me if you can."

Jon
P.S. Please don't try to call me. I won't answer any call.

She reads the brief note once, twice and then a third time. No, it doesn't sound like a joke. How come she has had absolutely no inkling that he has been so unhappy – so tired! The aroma of the percolating coffee hits her. On weekend mornings they always have their first cup together. In fact Jonathan makes it for both of them. He has always been the one rising earlier every morning including the weekends. It's odd to smell the freshly brewing coffee and not have him around.

Janet drops herself on the nearest chair and looks at the note one more time. Why? Why? What the hell is wrong with him? Is it another woman? Impossible! The lovemaking last night was memorable – in fact more than memorable, the best ever. The smell of their night together is wrapping her existence still. She is so used to it that she calls it Jon-smell. From under the corner chair his slippers are staring at her. They are positioned in a seventy- five-degree angle away from each other. He must have kicked them off before changing into his shoes, another of his familiar habits. Has he taken a suitcase or a backpack? She runs to the hallway closet to check the overhead shelf. Nothing seems to be missing. Then he must have brought up one of the suitcases from the basement. Oh no, he really left. A sudden throbbing headache began on her left temple, the spot where her monthly migraine appears. This is only the middle of the monthly cycle.

Perhaps he has just heard of a diagnosis of an incurable disease and he needs to get away to think, doesn't want to worry the family. But how could that be! His physical and all the blood works were done only a month ago and Janet has seen the reports. Janet sits there looking with blank eyes. She knows what she is doing. She is racking her brain to make some sense of this totally irrational behavior. It's so unlike Jon, the paragon of sensibility and reasons.

Janet pours the coffee in Jon's empty mug but cannot bring it to her lips. Tears of anger begin to burn her eyes. She lets them roll down her cheeks and to her robe collar. Thank goodness the girls are away spending the weekend with their grandmother in the next town. What will she tell Jonathan's mother? And the girls? "Dad needs a break from us. He'll be back when he's ready." "Damn you, Jon. Damn you, damn you." All the frustrations of twenty years which had been effectively buried by marital love and duty now surface. Flow of tears comes down like a spring mountain stream. She gets up to fetch a box of tissue; tears drop into the mug of coffee. 'Damn' she takes the mug to the sink and empties it. On second thought, she picks it up and throws it against the locked kitchen door leading to the back porch. She jumps to avoid being hit by a flying piece of ceramic. A broken moon-face stares up from the floor. Thank God nobody is home. She dries her tears on a kitchen towel, opens the refrigerator and closes it again. How can she eat anything!

Janet decides to go upstairs and change. A shower is what she needs right now. As she turns toward the staircase she stumbles on to one of his abandoned T-shirts. She kicks it in the same direction as the broken mug. At the head of the stairs where she turns to go to the master bedroom, she notices the large watercolor – a seascape they bought on a trip to Cape Cod one summer. Jon liked it and when he asked Janet if they should buy it, she looked at the price tag and said, 'No.' Jonathan spent one full hour trying to bring the price down and finally the owner of that little gallery agreed to sell it for 1700 dollars instead of 2500. The painting has become a conversation piece not so much for its artistic quality but the story of Jonathan's haggling skill. Janet knows how much Jon liked the piece. He'd say that looking at this vast blue of the ocean gives him such peace that he doesn't need to go to the Cape ever again. Janet often tells her dinner guests that the 1700 dollar-painting is the best investment they've ever made since they no longer need to go for a holiday. She smiles inadvertently at the memory and momentarily forgets what has happened.

In the shower Janet allows ice cold water to penetrate her skin, her hair, her being. She knows that sooner than later she'll have to act, do something. She doesn't know what yet. After the shower as she enters her bedroom she sees the unmade bed from last night. Jonathan's terry robe hangs from the hook behind the door. She goes to their walk-in closet, quickly picks up a pair of blue jeans and a cotton top avoiding looking at Jon's side of the closet. As she opens the top drawer of the dresser to get some fresh underwear, their wedding picture sitting on top of the dresser stares back at her. She picks it up, holds it in her two hands and wipes the glass tenderly. She has glanced at this photo everyday several times a day for last twenty years, yet never quite noticed her youthful innocent face. She lies down on the unmade bed with her wet hair holding and looking at her face on the wedding photo now. The off-white silk dress was not fashionable at the time. But she loved it. She loved herself in it. She can still smell the sterling roses in her wreath she wore around her cropped brown hair. She looks like an innocent angel, who has now fallen. How easy it is not to even look at the man standing next to her. No tears come flowing down this time. She stays this way for a long time until she feels a pang of hunger.

Janet gets up, puts the picture back to its place, dresses quickly and runs down to the kitchen to have breakfast. She decides to make bacon, eggs and toast, something she hasn't had since college days. She takes out the china, a wedding present from her best friend in college, and relishes her coffee in the bone china cup. A ribbon of morning sun floats on the golden liquid. As she drinks the sunny coffee, she talks to invisible Jonathan,

'Thank you, thank you for showing me the way. I too need a break. Take your time as I intend to take mine.'

The Swimmer of Colombo

Raising his head out of the water momentarily, Sunil Parera sees the white woman swimming vigorously from the other side. As she approaches, he dives underwater to make room for her. He has a glimpse of her wet blond hair that resembles the color of polished teak wood, the best available in his country. He covers the length of the pool quickly with powerful strokes and stops to see if his friends have come. At the other end, the young woman gets out of the pool and walks to the diving board preparing to jump, her firm breasts held in the bikini-top, slim legs poised to take off. From where he stands she looks like a crane about to fly. She dives smoothly and swims gracefully underwater like a shark and turns around.

Before independence from the British Empire, in the late 1950s this club belonged exclusively to the white population of Colombo, Sri Lanka. Now anyone can be a member. Knowing about Sunil's passion for swimming, the manager of the hotel, where Sunil supplies octopus, arranged a membership for him to this upscale club. Sunil, however, prefers to swim in the ocean. He comes to the pool only when heavy rains or storms prevent him from getting into the ocean.

Watching the girl, Sunil tries to imagine how this half-naked, long-legged white creature would look in the lapis-blue water of the Indian Ocean. He closes his eyes and sees his coal black body swimming side by side hers, while swarms of red, blue and yellow fishes slide around them. The daydream appears and disappears in a few seconds. He opens his eyes and sees the girl going out of the pool. She looks back momentarily and throws a brief smile at him.

A wave of electric pleasure runs through Sunil's veins. He climbs slowly out of the pool and limps toward the diving board. He wants to dive, no matter how hard it is for him. Right now anything is possible. A beautiful woman's smile is enough to rejuvenate the atrophied muscles of his back. The woman looks back and as she sees his deformed body her smile vanishes, and a frown appears between her brows. Sunil has seen this look in women's faces many times before. It's a mixture of disgust, repugnance and hate, as if they wish him to disappear from the face of the earth. His pleasure of a minute ago is rapidly replaced by a dark rage. He manages to jump from the board and swims vigorously across. Out of respectful fear the other swimmers quickly move aside. After a few minutes of swimming, Sunil calms down, rises from the pool and walks toward the shower room.

After the shower, Sunil looks at his naked body in the long mirror of the locker room. At five feet tall, his head with a mop of curly black hair is disproportionately big. The dark complexion of his face is almost gray from the pock marks, which make shaving difficult, leaving the face covered with uneven stubble. A large forehead ends in two widely separated small eyes. He can't help noticing his snub nose and thick lips, which hang over a truncated chin. However, he quickly moves his eyes to his broad shoulders, muscular chest and two strong arms. This makes the torso look more disproportionate because of his shrunken hip and legs. The left leg is a couple of inches shorter than the right.

Sunil looks at himself and almost feels sorry for the white girl. He knows that all his life this ugly deformity has kept women away from him. His own mother died immediately after his birth, perhaps because she could not tolerate looking at him. Sunil never found out who his father was. His nearly blind grandmother brought him up. Sometimes he wonders if she could see him clearly, would she have loved him!

The only person who was not aware of his ugliness was his school-mate Rani, who became his friend when they were in the fourth grade. They sat side by side, laughed and made mischief together. Sunil never saw the reflection of his ugliness in her eyes. To Rani he was as normal as the next boy or girl. When he was with her he forgot all about his disfigured body. Their friendship deepened over the next two years. Then one day Rani stopped coming to school. A week later, the Headmaster came to the class and announced that Rani had died from a virulent type of malaria. That day Sunil went to the ocean, sat near the water and cried for a long time. He wanted to die and follow his friend to that unknown place where no one would notice his deformity. But he could not leave his old grandmother alone. That was the day he swam in the ocean for the first time.

Sunil dresses and limps out of the club in a hurry. He heads toward the small café where he and his friends gather regularly. He wonders why his male friends have never left him because of his ugly looks. In fact, they seem eager to be near him, feeling elated if Sunil pays attention to them. They have nothing but admiration for his abilities in the water and his skill in spearing octopuses. Yet, Sunil cannot think of a single male friend to whom he can tell his deepest thoughts and bare his soul. How he would love to tell someone about his anger, shame and sadness.

The only time he is free of such heavy feelings is when he swims in the ocean. The salt water is his closest friend, whose embrace makes him forget how ugly and deformed he looks. The ocean takes his body in her arms like his lost mother. The water creatures consider him as one of them. The fish play with him. Sunil is restless only when he spots an octopus. All his anger and aggression gather in the muscles of his arms and he does not rest until he spears one. Even as a boy Sunil knew how to hunt octopus and with age he has perfected his skill. He supplies his catch to the local hotels. Apparently, this ugly tangled creature is a delicacy to some foreign tourists. A boat, a net, a couple of spears and an icebox are his tools for his successful business. He spends a big part of whatever money he makes on his friends. He always picks up the tab for their coffee and beer.

At dawn before the first ray of sun is visible Sunil rows his little boat out in the ocean. He anchors, and spears a dozen octopuses before putting them safely in the icebox. Then he rests by floating on the water and swimming for awhile. In the evening, he swims out again in the ocean where the waves catch the pink red reflection of the setting sun. He loves the red water, which reminds him of his anger. He feels light and free and swims as far as he can go. There in the distance, the ocean is emerald green, and underneath are colonies of coral, which are gray with orange and blue dots. Tiny flat fish with rainbow colors swim around the rugged coral ridges. Watching the underwater beauty makes Sunil feel part of this exquisite world.

In the depth of the Indian Ocean around the island of Sri Lanka, the rare gray corals with blue and orange dots are highly prized treasures. Many investors have tried to tempt Sunil to help them hunt these ridges of coral. He could be a rich man overnight, they promised him. Sunil paid no heed. He knew that these entrepreneurs would not stop. They would bring in tools and equipment from Australia and acquire their fortune by ravishing these beautiful creatures of the deep. Until that happens, this is his own personal world – no other human being has been here. This is Sunil's recluse, his sanctuary. If he cannot go there one day due to a storm or any other reason, he aches all over.

The next day, it has rained since early morning. A gale force wind from the Southwest has hit the city. The coconut groves along the coast keep swaying slapping over one another like drunken dancers. But they do not snap; their balanced resilience defies all odds. Waves as high as two storey- buildings crash on the shoreline. The fishermen have tied their boats to the iron poles and have left for the safety of their homes. Sunil waits two whole days for the storm to stop. When by the third day there is no sign of respite, he begins to pace like a wild animal in a cage. On the fourth day when the storm seems to have subsided a bit, he puts on his old raincoat and walks briskly toward Colombo Club. At least he can swim in the pool there. He will go stark crazy if he cannot swim for still one more day. The club is empty.

The bartender on the other side of the counter is leafing through an old magazine. The pool is nearly empty except for a few teenagers splashing water at one another. For some reason Sunil suddenly loses his desire to go into the pool. He sits at the bar and orders a beer. The bartender makes a few comments about the relentless weather. Without any response Sunil looks around. A couple has just entered and sits at a corner table. Sunil immediately recognizes the girl with blond hair. Her companion is a Sri Lankan man whom Sunil has never seen before. The young man appears to be quite tall, his complexion is a smooth mixture of gold and copper and his dark sleek hair is brushed back from a shapely forehead. He is wearing a short-sleeve cotton shirt, the top buttons of which are open. A pair of new sneakers is visible under the legs of his well-fitted jeans.

Sunil takes his second bottle of beer and moves to a different table from where he can easily see them. He pulls the chair hard making extra noise to attract attention. The young woman looks up. Sunil is sure that she recognizes him. The frown of the first day they met, appears between her brows again. Her companion, in the meantime, has gone to the counter to buy some drinks. Sunil smiles as he raises his beer bottle to greet her. The girl immediately moves her chair and turns her head away from Sunil's direction. A knife enters his chest.

The young man returns, passing by Sunil's table, carrying two cups of coffee. He leaves a whiff of expensive aftershave in the air. Sunil's anger now rises rapidly. From the corner of his eye he watches the girl whispering something to her companion. Sunil gets up and goes to the bar and buys another bottle of beer. He kicks a chair that's on his way. The girl has moved her chair and now sits next to the young man resting her head on his shoulder. Sunil is furious at their total disregard of decency in a public place. Has the man from his country lost his senses just because he is with a white girl? Sunil clutches the glass of beer hard to control his desire to punch his face into a pulp. The glass cracks into pieces and falls on the floor.

The girl lets out a scream when she sees Sunil's bloody hand. The young man helps her rise from her chair and guides her toward the door. Sunil cannot help noticing a look of deep fear in the girl's eyes before they leave. The bartender comes up with a small broom and begins to gather up the pieces of glass. Without looking up he asks if Sunil needs anything for his hand. Sunil is quiet now. His rage of a minute ago has been replaced by shame and remorse. He walks out of the bar without a word.

Outside, the rains have stopped. As Sunil limps fast, all he can think of is the look of fear in the girl's eyes. All his life he has been used to seeing dislike, disgust and even hate, but never fear. Does his deformity make him as dangerous as a wild beast? He pays no attention to his bleeding hand. He puts it inside the pocket of his raincoat and walks as fast as he can toward the ocean.

Even if the storm has stopped the sky is still dark as if some one has spilled a bottle of black ink all over. The ocean water reflects the same deep darkness. Sunil knows that this respite is temporary, the rains will resume again. He stands on the shore and looks around, then peels his clothes off and jumps into his beloved ocean. The saltwater burns his cut hand for a few seconds, but he ignores it and swims forward with his eyes closed. Days of rainfall have cooled the water more than usual. To warm up he swims vigorously. The next time he opens his eyes he knows he has reached his favorite spot, where the beautiful corals lay underneath.

Sunil continues to swim. He sees nothing but the wide spread of dark water in front of him that promises peace. At some point he knows that he has come too far and he is too tired to swim back. His arms and legs are tired and numb. Sunil turns around on his back and looks at the shore where the lights of the city are miniscule stars. He is far away from the civilization that has kept him at arm's length all his life, and now people's disgust and fear can no longer touch him. The ocean encircles him and holds him like the mother he has never known.

That night the storm returns again. The next morning, the sun shows up after six long days of rain and wind. Two fishermen of Colombo find Sunil's body in the water not far from the shore.

Ideal Partner in the Nineteen-Seventies

Way before the T.V. host David Letterman's Top Ten list became popular, my college dorm mate Connie had one detailing the desirable traits of her future husband. He'll have to have at least seven of the ten qualities to attract her attention. And, for her to make a commitment to love and marry he'll need to possess all ten. True to her words, she produced the following list.

(1) He'll be 5 feet 11 inches tall making the difference between their heights only 4 inches.

(2) His complexion not too fair, hair light brown, not neatly combed, a bit longer than what's fashionable at the time; a hint of a dimple on one cheek that will appear when he smiles.

(3) A voice not too deep, not too shallow, but slightly gritty as if he's trying to swallow a spoonful of coarse Kosher salt.

(4) He has to be physically clean and dress appropriately for the occasion – no sneakers to the operas and concerts.

(5) He'll have a Master's or a Ph.D. in philosophy or literature and will be a professor preferably at a university or a respectable college.

(6) He has to know how to play at least one musical instrument, preferably piano or saxophone and must appreciate modern jazz.

(7) He'll propose to her within six months of their first date with a 2 karat pigeon-blood ruby just like her grandfather gave her grandmother.

(8) He'll enjoy going to the cinema to watch art and foreign films and afterwards take her out to a surprise supper at an Italian trattoria.

(9) He'll not turn on the television to watch sports except tennis, and only during the Wimbledon season.

(10) He'll remember to bring her favorite flowers at least once a month and other gifts for her birthday and their anniversary.

After reading the list I told her, "You are the snob queen of a fantasy planet. Tell me you are joking. This can't be serious."

"One hundred percent," she said. "I'm not going to compromise myself. I think I deserve to have a partner with every one of these qualifications."

"Good luck!" I said.

Twenty years later I was at our college reunion and met Joyce, one of my classmates who knew Connie well. When I asked her if Connie had come, she said she was not sure. She did know that Connie lived in a small town in New Jersey and was teaching at an elementary school.

"Do you know if she found the man of her dream?" I had to ask.

"As far as I know she is still single."

Spilled Coffee

As she passes the shop windows absentmindedly, it occurs to Ellen that everything seems to be the same. But she does not feel the same at all and she knows why. But she does not want to think about it. The same familiar shops, the same newspaper stand and even the two blue plastic buckets of carnations and roses with the tag "$8.50 a dozen" are in their usual places. The dusty windows reflect her walking appearance momentarily. She too looks very much the same. The whole world out there including herself seems totally unchanged. Yet her world is upside-down as if it went through an earthquake. Her initial shock upon discovering that her husband, to whom she has been married for twenty long years, has been having an affair with her closest friend, has subsided now. Her disbelief which quickly followed the shock is now replaced by the knowledge, if not the acceptance, of the truth. She wishes she could hang on to the disbelief a bit longer. The worst part of it is that she does not know what to do.

It is Julia who has been Ellen's confidant whenever she needed to talk to someone. Now she needs to talk to someone about Julia. The irony hits her harder than the double betrayal of her husband and her best friend. Robert, her husband, always supported her and participated in their joint ventures, be that the children's education or planning a vacation. Suddenly their interests are separate. Now she has to fight alone against the two closest people in her life. Or does this call for some other strategy? Oh god, she wishes she knew!

Her watch says 10:45. Her appointment with the hairdresser is not until 11:30. What can she do to get away from her obsessive thoughts, her despair? If only by some miracle, she could go back to the last month when everything was as usual. Or, was it? This last suspicion nearly catches her by surprise. No, no she must get away from this incessant brooding. Determined, she buys a copy of Vogue and walks into the nearest coffee-shop to distract herself with the fashion world for a while until she is ready for her appointment.

As she steps inside, the relatively darker atmosphere blinds her for a few seconds. She walks toward what looks like an empty booth and nearly trips on a handbag strap that is dangling from a seat. As she steadies herself Ellen sees Julia sitting right in front of her, alone. The last person Ellen expects to see right now is Julia, although Julia has been on her mind constantly for the last three weeks.

"Oh, hi, didn't see you. It's kind of dark in here after the bright sun outside. Are you alone? May I..." Ellen regrets her question as soon as she utters it. She only hopes Julia is not waiting for Robert. But Robert is supposed to be in New

Haven today. This is the first time that the two friends have not hugged each other on a chance meeting like this. Ellen sits down with a nervous smile and feels totally disoriented. This encounter is the last thing she anticipated and has prepared for.

"Sure, please," says Julia. "I see you've been shopping. Do you shop around here often? I would have thought it's a bit out of your way."

"No, yes it is, out of my way that is. My new hairdresser is in this area. I came early to pick up a few things. I still have some extra time. It's good to… Do you come here often yourself?" Ellen runs her fingers through her hair thinking she must look awful. She avoids Julia's eyes and looks around to catch the waitress'. Julia stirs her coffee slowly, her eyes averted.

Trying to guess Julia's thoughts Ellen says, "If you wanted to be alone I could move to another table… Oh, here you are at last" to the waitress. "I would like a cup of coffee, please. Black." She looks up and forgets what she has been saying before the waitress appeared. She wishes desperately for Julia to say something, anything which would rescue both of them from the present situation. Then, she realizes, Julia perhaps does not know that she knows. Ellen almost feels sorry for the woman sitting opposite her. She looks at her opponent, trying to see what many women before her tried to see. What has Julia to offer that Ellen does not? Ellen herself is astounded by this cliché she is falling into now. She looks at Julia and decides to be blunt and ask her directly about it. Instead, she asks if Julia would like another cup of coffee. Her hand shakes slightly as she fumbles inside her bag to find a hairbrush. Her hair must be a mess. Who likes to meet a friend just before going to a hairdresser? She says absentmindedly,

"Maybe I should let my hair grow again. Remember how the two of us one day decided to cut our hair short to surprise our husbands?" As soon as she lets these words spill out of her mouth she is so annoyed with herself that she barely misses hitting the extended hand of the waitress who is just about to put Ellen's cup of coffee in front of her. "Why don't we, the four of us go out for dinner or something. We used to do things together. What do you say?" This time she's ashamed by the insincerity of her own tone. Ellen gulped her coffee as if to stop herself from talking. Why can't Julia say something for a change? Ellen tries to drink her coffee quickly. In her rush she splashes some in the saucer. As she tries to grab a paper napkin the cup in her other hand tilts and pours most of its content on the table. "Oh no. Now what have I done!"

Julia jumps out of her seat trying to protect her cream-colored dress and bumps her head on the overhead metal lamp. The situation could be a bit comical under different circumstances, Ellen thinks. Together they manage to wipe most of the liquid before it reaches the floor or them. Julia summons the waitress for help. Ellen says quickly, "No, no I don't want any more, honestly. Let me see. Are you hurt? Here, put the wet napkin on it. You have a tiny bump." Julia takes the wet napkin that Ellen dipped into the glass of water and sits down looking at Ellen. Suddenly she begins to sob. Puzzled, Ellen asks, "Is it really that bad?" Ellen looks at her friend across the table and feels her own tears welling up inside her. She gets up, excusing herself, saying she needs to use the toilet. No, she must not let Julia see her tears.

As she rushes out of the coffee-shop on to the street her eyes are blinded again by the glare. Not until she starts her car does she remember that she has not paid for her coffee. She has not said goodbye to Julia either. She has not forgotten her appointment with the hairdresser. But she cannot bring herself to go there or anywhere. She turns her car off and sits for a long time. Tears that started in the coffee-shop now are falling without reserve.

Hunger Strike

"The patient in Room 106 A refused to eat all her meals for two days now." Nurse Maria Lopez reports to the attending physician of the cancer ward of Emerson Hospital as she catches up with him. Without slowing down his rapid steps the doctor says,

"Do something. Put a tube down her throat; whatever. I have to take care of other patients who have more urgent problems." He disappears around a corner before Maria can respond. The patient in question, Mrs. Polonski is an 85-year-old post-operative woman with stage 4 uterine cancer. Ever since her surgery three days back, she has refused to eat anything solid. Maria took interest in her because she knew the patient had no family and because she looks so sad. Mrs. Polonski reminds Maria of her grandmother who lives in Puerto Rico by herself. For two days Maria has tried hard to make the old woman eat without avail and her condition has deteriorated further.

The next morning skipping her own breakfast, Nurse Lopez takes out a tangerine form her lunch box and visits Mrs. Polonski. Peeling the tangerine neatly, she arranges the sections on a paper plate and offers them to the patient, who does not touch them. So the nurse sits quietly for a few minutes and eats a piece herself and pushes the plate toward Mrs. Polonsky, who opens her mouth to speak.

"Thanks, but I can't eat. I know you are trying to keep me alive. But I have no desire to live when I don't even know how Sam is doing." This surprises Nurse Lopez. She thought Mrs. Polonski had no relatives. Before she says anything, Mrs. Polonski asks her very gently, "Do you think you can dial a number for me? I need to know how Sam is doing. He may be starving too…" She can not finish her words. Tears choke her. Maria gets up and hands her a box of tissue. Now she knows that Sam must be a close friend or an ex-husband who is not mentioned in her medical report. Maria opens her cell phone and asks the patient for Sam's number.

When the phone rings the nurse hands the receiver to Mrs. Polonski. "Hello, hello, Nancy? It's me, Angela. How is my Sammy? Oh, good. Thank God, and thank you for feeding him. Bless your heart. Here, you talk to the nurse." As Mrs. Polonski hands the receiver over to Maria her old wet eyes smile and she picks up a section of the tangerine and chews it slowly. After talking to Mrs. Polonski's neighbor, Nurse Lopez calls the kitchen and orders a full breakfast for her patient. She holds Mrs. Polonski's hand, smiles at her and says,

"I'm so glad your Sam is being taken care of. Now let us take care of you." Mrs. Polonski takes her wallet from under the pillow and pulls out a photo of Sam and shows it to Maria.

This time the nurse's eyes become misty when she sees a dog's soulful eyes looking back at her.

The Wristwatch

After checking in my luggage, I still had over an hour before the flight to Boston. Geneva airport is fairly quiet on a Tuesday afternoon. I decided to get a few boxes of chocolate for gifts and turned to enter a duty-free shop. A slightly overweight woman of medium height and flushed reddish face asked me,

"Pardon, do you know if this is the general gate of departure for all flights?" Despite her haste she tried to smile. She had a pair of bright blue eyes framed by radiating crowfeet under a lined forehead. I saw a woman above sixty-five or seventy—dressed in a light lavender silk dress and leather pumps. Unsure of what she meant, I hesitated.

"I'm looking for a friend who is leaving for Tokyo this morning. You see I taught him French for two years. We're very close. I wonder if he'll go through this set of doors as everyone else." She asked in a hurry. Then looking around her face brightened. She spotted someone at the head of the escalator and ran toward him. Something in her voice and face made me change my mind about the duty-free shop and decided to watch them from a comfortable distance yet within ear-shot. I felt a twinge of guilt doing it, but argued with myself that one of the pleasures of traveling is to observe other passengers. I ignored the fact that I was eavesdropping.

With a travel bag on his shoulder, an Asian man from China or Japan around age fifty approached the security gates in rapid steps. The woman in the lavender dress stepped forward and grabbed his left arm with a big smile. The man's face showed no expression, not even a flicker of surprise.

"Here you are! I was so afraid I had missed you. I wanted to say a proper good bye." She opened her handbag and took out a narrow box wrapped in gold-colored paper and pushed it inside his coat pocket. He said nothing showing an impatient gesture to turn toward the gates. "I know you like Swiss watches. This is the best available. I hope you'll wear it and think of me a little." Her voice cracked slightly as her eyes filled with tears.

The man now appeared annoyed, looked at her for the first time and said something under his breath, which I could not hear. She ignored his words, raised herself to reach his face and kissed him on his lips. He immediately took out a handkerchief from his breast pocket and wiped his mouth and turned to go. The woman stepped back and held on to a counter for support. Tears rolled down her cheeks as she followed the departing man with her foggy eyes.

I refrained from an immediate urge to go to her and say or do something to console her. Not knowing anything about their story, I had no right to interfere with people's private business. After all, I just met the lady only for a couple of minutes. Noticing the time on the big clock above the door I too turned to go. All this took a few minutes.

By the time I got in the line for the passport control booth I noticed that I was two persons behind the Asian man on the queue. For some reason I felt compelled to keep my eyes on him.

I watched him adjust his shoulder bag, put his passport inside a side pocket of the shoulder bag, and adjust the strap across his chest diagonally. He used his free right hand inside his coat pocket and took out the narrow box wrapped in gold paper. Then he rushed toward a trash receptacle and dropped it as if the box contained some explosive.

I was relieved that by now we were not visible from outside the security area. I still looked back to make sure that the woman in the lavender silk dress and a pair of bright blue eyes was not watching. I saw only a row of busy travelers rushing toward their individual gates.

On board the plane I kept thinking of the woman and wondered what she could have done to be treated with such disgust. All through the long flight of nearly twelve hours I began to imagine one scenario after another culminating with the scene I witnessed. Finally, I gave up but felt that perhaps, in a small way, I was able to share a stranger's sorrow.

The Wheelchair

One Sunday morning as Rajat was leafing through the local newspaper, a small inset on the second page caught his eyes. *An Indian woman was crushed to death when her wheelchair fell into the deep gorge of the Grand Canyon. After their thorough investigation, the police concluded that this was an unfortunate accident.* After reading this terrible news Rajat sat quietly for several minutes. He could not shake off the shock although he had no idea who these people were. An avid reader of detective novels, he could not ignore the probability of foul play.

The next day Rajat received a number of e-mails at work from his college friends. All the e-mails bore the same news: The woman who died in the Grand Canyon accident happened to be the wife of their classmate Gourab Datta. This information delivered Rajat an additional blow, although Rajat knew Gourab only superficially. Gourab was a handsome athlete and a brilliant student. Rajat did not dare go close to someone like Gourab. But Rajat and his friends knew about him from the college gossips. All this happened twenty-five years ago. Rajat now recalled another piece of gossip that Gourab ended up marrying his high school sweetheart whose name was Sahana.

Rajat had been working for a small company in Fort Collins, Colorado and had been living there alone for fifteen years. He had never married. At forty-nine, the bachelor's life seemed to suit him well. He enjoyed hiking and skiing in the Rockies.

That night Rajat made a decision. After spending some time on Google Search, he found Gourab's telephone number and was surprised to see that Gourab's address was not far away. He left a voice mail saying that he was an old classmate and now lived in the same state. He was shocked to hear the horrible news and would be happy to visit if Gourab wanted his company. The very next day Rajat received an e-mail. It read, "I cannot say I remember your name. But I'm extremely grateful for your offer to come to be with me at the saddest time of my life. How about this Friday?" This surprised Rajat. He did not expect such a response at all. After contacting Gourab he began to get cold feet and was hoping to get out of this crazy plan somehow.

On Friday, Rajat packed a backpack and following Gourab's directions drove his old Land Rover to Gourab's lavish home on the slope of Flagstaff Hill in Boulder. It was late afternoon. Gourab stood at the gate—his six-foot height still imposing, although no longer as slim. His handsome face betrayed sleeplessness. Gourab showed Rajat where to park and picked up his backpack and walked inside.

"What a lovely home you have!" Rajat exclaimed.

"It was Sahana's choice. She wanted to live on the hill." Gourab said and quickly changed the topic, "Let me show you your room. Please follow me." They stopped in front of a well-furnished guest room. "Meet me on the deck after you wash up. What would you like? Beer? or wine?" Gourab said.

"Either is fine. Thanks."

A few minutes later Rajat found his host on the huge deck overlooking the eastern slope of Flagstaff reflecting the setting sun. He was pouring beer in a glass. Handing the glass to Rajat he poured another glass for himself. Gourab stretched his long legs above the railing and kept his eyes on the hill. No one talked for several minutes. Then keeping his eyes on the distant mountains Gourab talked.

"In case you're wondering why no one from my family came to console me, it is because I became estranged from them after my marriage." He got up moved his chair toward Rajat and made eye contact with him before continuing, "You're a Godsend. I needed a sympathetic soul with whom I could talk openly. If I were Christian, I could go to a confessor." Rajat was surprised by this last statement and looked directly at Gourab, who continued, "Before I tell you anything you have to give me your word that you will never utter a single word to anyone. Even though I do not know you well, something tells me that I can trust you."

"All right, I give my word." Rajat said slowly. His curiosity got the better of him. The sun had set in the meantime and the evening darkness began to envelope them. Gourab got up from his chair, went inside and came back with a plate of cold roasted chicken and a long French bread. He poured more beer in their glasses and began to talk again.

"Over thirty years ago I saw Sahana for the first time in a sports competition at the girls' high school of our town. She was the fastest runner of the hundred-meter sprint. I still remember vividly the straight line formed between her hair and toes making a thirty-degree angle with the ground. Her long legs seemed ready to fly just like the flying cranes in the autumn sky. Her running speed made the whole picture a blurry apparition. That was the moment when I felt a strong attraction to her, or should I say to her running legs!

Not just the hundred-meter sprint, Sahana Bose won first prize in all kinds of sports that year. And I was first in many of the events from the boys' high school. Soon afterwards, because of my fame as a student athlete, I had no problem winning Sahana's heart. Two years after that we both joined the same engineering college. After graduation, we got married and got jobs in the same city. We did not have kids even in ten years of marriage because I did not want any children and Sahana accepted my decision. Then suddenly at age forty Sahana contacted polio!" Gourab stopped, cleared his throat and continued,

"The ethereal beauty of the fastest moving legs which made me fall in love with her in the first place now lost their mobility. Since then, for fifteen years, I have nursed her and pushed her wheelchair to the best clinics of the world. No treatment helped. Sahana learned to accept this tragic fate and never complained. But I could not accept it. I could never forget the most beautiful apparition of running Sahana, the first time I saw her and fell in love. How could I accept the wheelchair-bound existence for the queen of my dreams, who could run like the fastest cheetah! Finally, I succumbed to my obsession without a single thought of the consequences." Gourab finished his confession.

Rajat was speechless. He looked away and saw the dark shadow of the moon on the distant waves of the mountains. He shivered inside thinking that now he was honor-bound to keep a horrible secret.

CPSIA information can be obtained
at www.ICGtesting.com
Printed in the USA
JSHW021101030223
37163JS00001B/64